River Run Series Book Three

By M. L. Bullock

Text copyright © 2024 Monica L. Bullock

All rights reserved.

Contents

Chapter One—Wen 4
Chapter Two–Kim 15
Chapter Three–May 22
Chapter Four–Kim 34
Chapter Five–Wen 47
Chapter Six–Sophia 58
Chapter Seven–Kim 67
Chapter Eight–May 76
Chapter Nine–David Ray 88
Chapter Ten–May 106
Chapter Eleven–David 118
Chapter Twelve–May 126
Chapter Thirteen–Wen 139
Epilogue–Carmen 156
Author's Note 160
M. L. Bullock's Book List 162

Chapter One—Wen

As we drove up the winding path that led to our new home, I couldn't help but be captivated by the grandeur of River Run. The realtor hadn't lied at all. This place was perfect.

The estate, cloaked in ivy and shadowed by towering oaks, stood as a monument to a bygone era, its once magnificent façade now marred by time and neglect. The setting sun cast an eerie glow through the branches, bathing the house in an amber light that seemed both welcoming and foreboding.

I knew old houses weren't my wife's cup of tea, but she was pretty agreeable about such things. I didn't glance over at her; I didn't want to see the disappointment on her face. Nobody spoke as we parked the car and walked up the steps to our new home.

Despite the charm, a shiver coursed through me as we crossed the threshold of the great wooden door, its creaks sounding like the whispers of the long departed.

It was a chill that seemed to seep into my very bones, a cold whisper from the unseen. In that moment, I felt an omen—an inexplicable warning that this place held secrets darker than its shadowed corners suggested.

Yet, as I looked back at May and Kim, my daughter's face alight with a mix of excitement and awe, I chose to ignore the dread that tugged at my instincts. At least she was excited about living in an American historical home.

This was to be our new beginning, and I could not let my unease cloud our first moments in River Run.

As the last slivers of daylight faded, giving way to the encroaching twilight, our new home seemed to settle around us with an almost audible sigh, as if it too was weary from standing guard over its long-kept secrets.

Strangely enough, I believed that. Felt it deep in my bones. It was right that we were here. Right? Suddenly, I wasn't so sure. Wow, that flipped on a dime.

Amid the sea of boxes and furniture that now cluttered the living room, I stumbled upon an unexpected relic. Tucked away in a crevice of the stone fireplace, hidden beneath years of dust and neglect, was an old book. Its leather cover was cracked and worn; the pages yellowed with age.

Curiosity piqued, I carefully opened it, the musty scent of paper filling my nostrils. The faded handwriting was difficult to decipher, but it spoke of events long past, of whispers and cries muffled by the thick walls of River Run.

As I leafed through the pages, a chill ran down my spine—not from the cold, but from the realization that these walls had indeed witnessed more than their fair share of sorrow.

Later, as we continued to unpack in uneasy silence, May's voice broke through the monotony, her tone tinged with a nervous edge.

"Do you feel that, Wen? It's like... like we're being watched." Her eyes darted around the dimly lit room, seeking confirmation of her unease. "I don't see any cameras and there aren't any open curtains or blinds, but I can't shake the feeling."

I looked up from the antique book, meeting her gaze. It was easy to attribute her feelings to the stress of the move and the strangeness of our new surroundings.

"It's just being in a new place, love," I reassured her, forcing a smile. "And maybe our minds are playing tricks after a long day. Look at this. I found a treasure although I can barely read it. Come on, let's find food and get settled for the night. It's getting late."

I wanted to believe my own words, that everything was great and fine. I wanted to dismiss the uneasy feeling that had settled in the pit of my stomach, but as I glanced back at the old book, I couldn't shake the feeling that there was some truth hidden in May's instinctive unease.

Yet, for the sake of our new start, I pushed the strange thoughts aside, resolving to focus on the tangible tasks at hand.

Geesh. I sound like my Goldie. She claimed to see spookies, as she called them, in every corner of our home and village. If she were alive, I wonder what she'd think of this place.

As the night deepened, the only illumination within the walls of River Run came from the sporadic flicker of candles and the weak glow of a single overhead light. *What was wrong with the wiring in this place? Add that to the list of things that needed to be fixed.*

I headed down to the basement, flashlight in hand, May nagged me from the top stop. Like usual. We never communicated anymore. She nagged and I pretended not to hear her. So far, it worked but for how long?

I waved the beam of light around and found the breaker box. Sure enough, many of the breakers had been flipped. I flipped them back and breathed a sigh of relief when the lights came on and the hum of electricity filled the hold house.

Okay. Maybe it won't be too bad.

Feeling victorious after figuring that situation out, I focused on arranging our belongings, but my efforts were repeatedly thwarted by fleeting movements at the edge of my vision. May was often in the room with me but didn't seem to notice the odd movements, so I didn't bring it up to her.

I did however once or twice catch my daughter Kim's eyes following the shadows as they moved. She looked at me, but I only shrugged. I had no answers for her. None at all. Better to ignore the strangeness.

Shadows seemed to dart and dance along the periphery, slipping into the corners of the room as soon as I turned to look. I told myself it was merely the light playing tricks, the natural consequence of tired eyes in an old house with wind-worn windows and creaking floors.

Yet, the frequency of these glimpses left me uneasy, a nagging doubt whispering that perhaps not all was as it seemed.

Later, when I retreated to the small room that would serve as my office, the sensation of intrusion overwhelmed me. May walked in with a box of my things, placed it on my desk and immediately left. My wife used to smile all the time. It had been a long time since I'd seen that beautiful smile. I had no one to blame by myself.

It had been one indiscretion. One. How long was she going to punish me?

As I set up my desk, placing my computer and design books in their new spots, I couldn't shake the feeling that I was not alone. *May was right.* It was as if the air around me was charged, heavy with the presence of someone—or something—watching my every move.

The room was cold, unnaturally so, and the hairs on the back of my neck stood on end. I tried to focus on arranging my designs, to lose myself in the familiar lines and colors, but the sensation of eyes boring into my back was relentless.

"May? Is that you?" I called out into the hallway, but she didn't answer me. I stepped into the hall. There was no one there.

Despite my skepticism, a voice inside me insisted that this discomfort was more than mere paranoia. It was as if the house itself was aware of my family's presence, and perhaps not entirely welcoming us.

I paused, my hands hovering over the messy desk and slowly turned to survey the room.

Nothing appeared amiss, yet the feeling of being observed persisted. With a deep, uncertain breath, I turned back to my work of setting up my gear, determined to ignore the unease that clung to me like a second skin, but the shadows in my mind were not so easily dismissed.

Man, this is getting worse and worse.

As night enveloped River Run, the whisper of dusk seemed to breathe a life of its own into the house. The air grew denser, charged with an intangible whisper that echoed faintly through the hallways.

That's when I heard the voices. Soft, whispery, difficult to hear.

I paused, a shiver running down my spine as I strained to listen. The sounds were elusive, like murmured secrets just beyond the edge of understanding, rising and falling with the wind that moaned against the ancient window frames.

Compelled by a mix of fear and determination, I followed the whispers down the creaking corridors, my footsteps silent on the worn carpet.

Each room I checked was bathed in shadows, empty yet thick with anticipation, as if the house itself was holding its breath. I flipped the light switches on in every room. They all worked but the lights did nothing to shake off the heaviness.

No source for the whispers could be found, yet the unsettling chorus did not cease. It was as if the very walls were speaking, recounting tales lost to time, meant only for the dead—or perhaps the damned—to hear.

May passed me in the hallway, another box in her hand. Her eyes did not meet mine. I didn't ask but I hoped she would room with me. Since my brief affair, she'd taken to sleeping in the guest room but that was at the old house. Maybe here, at River Run, she'd change her mind.

Maybe. I didn't want to push her. I was just grateful that I talked her out of divorce. But I'd quit the job, avoided Carly and even allowed my wife to confront her old friend.

As we all prepared for bed, the atmosphere was taut with the residue of the day's discoveries and the night's eerie serenade. Kim, sensing the change, approached me, her eyes wide and troubled in the dim light of her new room.

"Daddy, I don't like these noises," she whispered, her voice quivering slightly as another groan swept through the house, like the sigh of a weary spirit. "Can you hear them?"

I knelt beside her bed, smoothing her hair back with a reassuring hand. "It's just the house settling, sweetheart," I murmured, my voice steady despite the unease that clawed at my own chest. "Every old house makes strange sounds, especially really old ones like this. We'll all get used to it soon, I promise."

Her small nod, more an act of trust than conviction, pulled at my heart.

"Daddy?"

"Yes, Kim?"

"Can you hang my prayer streamer? The one Goldie made me?" Goldie had been my grandmother's nickname. I smiled at her.

"Of course, honey. Where did you put it?"

"It's in the box in the closet I asked Mommy but I think she forgot," she sounded a bit whiny but who could blame her.

I opened the closet and caught my breath. On the other side of the retinue of boxes was a tall shadow of a man. I pulled the light chain, and he was gone. Or whatever it was had vanished. I quickly shuffled through the boxes and found the painted sutras and found a small container of push pins.

I quickly turned off the light and closed the closet door, my hands shaking my heart thumping. I prayed that my daughter hadn't seen what I'd seen.

Get it together, Wen. This was your idea. Your dream home.

She said nothing about it but told me where to hang the banners. I did so gladly. Together we prayed and she settled into sleep. I glanced at the closet and was tempted to look once more but why risk it?

I probably imagined it. Guilt manifesting as shadows.

As I left her room, the soft click of the door sounding unnaturally loud, the whispered voices seemed to hush, as if curious about the new lives unfolding within these storied walls.

I was relieved to see May making our bed and already in her pajamas. Most of the work of organizing the house would be done tomorrow but at least we'd be here together. I tried not to smile and make a big deal out of it. No way was I going to push it.

She sighed a few times but never said anything. She didn't complain but the sighs themselves were complaints.

Eventually we both settled into an uneasy sleep, the silence that followed not quite comforting, laden as it was with the heavy breath of River Run, waiting, watching.

Watching and waiting.

We wouldn't have long to wait.

Chapter Two—Kim

The night was late and the moon hung low outside my window, casting eerie shadows across my new room. I used to like looking at the moon and stars at night but not here. Not at River Run.

Everything was quiet, too quiet, like the world was holding its breath. I lay in my bed, clutching my favorite blanket tightly, trying to find comfort in its familiar softness.

Above me, the colorful prayer streamers Daddy had hung fluttered suddenly, as if touched by an unseen hand. I watched, wide-eyed, as the papers moved back and forth, the painted sutras dancing in a silent rhythm. I worried for a moment that someone, someone invisible would tear them down.

Thankfully, that didn't happen.

My heart started to beat faster, the quiet around me now filled with the soft rustling of the streamers. I tried to tell myself it was just the wind, but the windows were closed, and the air in the room felt still and heavy, like it was thick with whispers. The fluttering of the banners seemed to grow more frantic, and I felt a cold dread seeping into my bones.

Suddenly, from under the door, smoke began to pour into the room. It was thin at first, like morning fog, but soon it swelled into thick, choking clouds. I couldn't understand where it was coming from. There was no smell of fire, just a cold, damp scent that made the hairs on the back of my neck stand up.

Panic gripped me, and I scrambled out of bed, my feet hitting the cold floor as I stood frozen for a moment.

"Mommy! Daddy!" I screamed, my voice shrill with terror. The smoke swirled around my ankles, creeping higher as if it were alive. I backed away from the door, my eyes wide, watching as the smoke filled the room, casting everything in a ghostly haze.

My heart thudded painfully in my chest as I waited, desperate for the sound of my parents rushing to my rescue.

The dense, swirling smoke seemed to muffle my screams, absorbing the sound as it enveloped me. I stood frozen, my little voice lost amidst the creeping fog that filled my room.

Why couldn't Mommy and Daddy hear me?

The thought terrified me more than the smoke itself. My chest tightened with fear, and I couldn't move, my feet as if glued to the floor. I felt so small, so helpless in the vast, shadowy space of my new room.

Then, as suddenly as it had appeared, the smoke began to dissipate, thinning into wisps before vanishing completely.

I was left standing in the cold silence, my heart still pounding in my chest. A chill breeze brushed against my skin, making me shiver. It seemed to whisper through the room, rustling the streamers again. With a quick, frightened glance around, I dashed back to my bed, diving under my favorite blanket for any sense of security I could find.

The quiet returned, but it was a heavy, watchful silence.

As my eyes adjusted to the dim light, I noticed something even more terrifying. My toys, my precious collection of Asian blessing dolls that Goldie had given me, seemed different.

Their usual cheerful expressions looked strange and ominous in the flickering shadow of the nightlight. I stared at them, my breath caught in my throat, and then, all at once, they turned to face me. I couldn't understand how; I hadn't touched them.

A scream tore from my lungs, louder and more frantic than before. This time, the sound pierced the eerie stillness, and within moments, the door burst open. Light flooded the room as Mommy rushed to my side, her face etched with concern.

"What's wrong, Kimmy? What happened?" she asked, her voice soothing yet laced with worry.

I pointed at the dolls, now innocuously still, their faces serene as if mocking my fear. "They... they looked at me," I sobbed, clinging to her as she gathered me into her arms.

Mommy looked over at the dolls, then back at me. She didn't seem to see what I saw, but she didn't doubt my fear.

"It's okay, baby. You're safe now," she murmured, rocking me gently. "Let me close the cabinet for the night. Let them go to sleep too." She rose from the bed and walked over to the cabinet and closed the doors.

I breathed a sigh of relief. Mommy returned to sit beside me. Her presence calmed me, but as I nestled against her, the cold dread lingered, a silent reminder that River Run was full of shadows not yet understood.

"Mommy? Will you stay with me?" I pleaded as I tugged my favorite blanket up under my chin.

"Of course, baby. Scootch over." I gladly did that. Soon she was asleep and snoring. Not me. I wasn't sure if I would ever sleep again.

The night wore on, the moon casting long shadows across the room where Mommy and I lay.

Just as I began to feel the tug of weary sleep, a faint giggle pierced the silence. It was light, carefree—a sound that should have been comforting, but under the cloak of darkness, it was chilling.

I lifted my head, scanning the room with wide eyes. The corners remained empty, the spaces under the furniture clear. There was no other child there, just the echoes of a laugh that seemed to come from nowhere. I had no siblings and there were no neighbor kids, as far as I knew.

My heart raced as I huddled closer to Mommy, but she was deep in sleep, undisturbed by the sounds that haunted me.

Determined to prove I wasn't imagining things, I slowly slid out from under the blanket and tiptoed to the doorway. The hall was dimly lit by the night lights, casting eerie, elongated shadows against the walls.

That's when I noticed them—small, wet footprints on the wooden floor. They led towards the bathroom, the little puddles reflecting the moonlight. Those weren't my footprints. I'd taken a bath hours ago.

With a mixture of fear and curiosity, I followed the footprints, my own bare feet cold against the floor. Each step felt heavier as I approached the bathroom door, which was ajar.

Pushing it open, I peeked inside. The room was empty. No one was there. The wet footprints just ended abruptly by the bathtub. My breath caught in my throat, and I quickly ran back to my room, the giggling still ringing in my ears.

I ran back to my room as fast as I could. Despite jumping in the bed, I didn't wake up Mommy. She must be exhausted.

The next morning, I told Mommy about what happened—the giggling child and the wet footprints leading to an empty bathroom.

She listened, her brows furrowed with concern, but her eyes didn't quite believe the tales of phantom children and invisible laughs.

"It was just a dream, Kim, a bad dream," she said softly, trying to soothe my fears.

"But it wasn't, Mommy! I saw it... I heard her!" I protested, feeling the sting of being disbelieved.

Mommy sighed, kissing my forehead. "Try to get some rest today, okay? It's been a big move, and sometimes our minds play tricks on us when we're tired. At least that's what your father says."

Feeling brushed aside, I nodded, but the unease didn't leave me.

After a day of unpacking boxes and eating a boring meal, night fell again. I lay in my bed, the image of the little dead girl I had imagined at the end of those wet footprints haunting me. I could almost imagine her perfectly.

She seemed so real, so sad, trapped in whatever limbo held her to River Run.

My eyes stayed wide open, staring at the dark ceiling as I listened for sounds that no one else seemed to hear. The shadows felt closer, more oppressive, as if waiting for something—or someone—to acknowledge their presence.

And in the depth of the night, I wondered if I was the only one who could see the sadness woven into the fabric of our new home.

Somehow, I knew I wasn't. Soon, we would all know the truth.

We were not alone.

Chapter Three–May

Each day in our new home left me feeling a tension that seemed woven into the very fabric of the house. I'd never been one to be superstitious, but here, at River Run, I found myself tossing salt over my shoulder. I reminded Kim not to whistle in the house after dark. No need to draw any unwanted supernatural attention.

Wen raised his eyebrow when I reminded him to take the trash out before dark. That was another tradition I grew up with in my mother's home. Garbage and untidiness attracted imps and goblins. Goldie, as my daughter liked to call my late mother, was always full of such illogical wisdom.

Suddenly, I was now saying the same things.

As I moved through the silent corridors and shadowed rooms, a sense of sorrow hung heavily in the air, like the remnants of whispered grief caught in the lace curtains.

I never wanted to come here. I didn't even want to be married anymore but divorce was out of the question. I took my vows seriously, despite my very flawed husband.

I'd not finished college even though I was only a year from finishing my accounting degree.

Wen had been so eager to marry and start a family. Me too, at the time but it had been a huge mistake. I had Kim to think about.

I could never have imagined that my plain-faced, mildly intelligent husband would cheat on me. Why come home and tell me about it? To make himself feel better, that's why. And in doing so, he'd robbed me of my joy, of our happy family.

But if he wanted to pretend that all was well, I could do that too. I'd already made up my mind. I was going to get my degree and when Kim was old enough to understand my decision, Wen and I were through.

I kept my anger to myself, but I kept it close and would not allow myself to show Wen any softness.

Sometimes, when I was alone, the feelings of betrayal and anger intensified. Strangely enough, since moving to River Run these thoughts invited strange activity. Like a cold brush against my skin, ever so lightly, or a sigh in the quiet of the empty house that made my heart skip.

The house, with its creaking floors and drafts that seemed to whisper through the walls, carried a chill that settled deep in my bones.

I hated this house. Why here?

I tried to dismiss the strange touches and cold spots as just the settling of an old structure or the wind carving its way through hidden cracks, but the heaviness was palpable, almost as if the sadness of the house was a tangible thing, trying to seep deeper into my troubled spirit.

I would often pause in my daily chores, feeling the weight of unseen eyes upon me, the air thick with a history that was both unknown and familiar.

It was during these moments of quietude, amidst the solitude of my new surroundings, that the house revealed its true nature—not merely as a structure of wood and stone, but as a keeper of secrets, of stories that needed to be heard.

The more time I spent alone—and I craved being alone--the more I felt the presence of something—or someone—lingering just out of sight. It was as if the house itself was alive, watching and waiting, its breath a whisper against the back of my neck.

One chilly afternoon, as I was arranging and dusting the library, a room seldom used and thick with the musty scent of old books and forgotten tales, the air shifted around me.

I couldn't understand why Wen hadn't claimed this room as his office so I did. There were plenty of rooms in this colonial two story home. Too much space, in my opinion.

Suddenly, a cold draft swept through the room, rustling the pages of an open tome on the desk, its words a blurred echo of past lives. I shivered, pulling my cardigan tighter around my shoulders. I drew closer and tried to decipher the writing but my English was not great, especially since the ink appeared to be vanishing before my eyes. I closed the book. Surely, that was a trick of the light.

Where was this cold coming from?

I reached to close the window I thought I had left open, my hand paused in mid-air—the window was already shut.

I stepped back, its latch covered in a fine layer of undisturbed dust. Confusion rippled through me, a cold finger traced down my spine.

"Wen?" I whispered hopefully. Turning slowly, my eyes scanned the shadowed shelves and heavy furniture, half-expecting to see my husband or daughter. But there was only silence—a heavy, expectant silence that seemed almost to breathe.

That's when I felt it—a palpable sense of sadness washing over me, so intense it was nearly suffocating. The room seemed to darken, the shadows deepening into corners so black they appeared endless.

My heart pounding, I was about to flee the room when I saw her—a girl, no older than a child in a fairy tale, standing by the window. Her dress was a faded remnant from another century, her small face framed by golden curls that shimmered faintly in the dim light.

Her eyes met mine, and the sadness in them was almost too much to bear. She didn't speak, but her gaze conveyed a mournful knowledge of tragedies long past.

Poor child. What happened to you?

Her presence was so palpable, so vivid, that I stood frozen, a dusting cloth still in hand, as she slowly faded away like mist. I waited for an answer but she did not speak.

Instead, she touched the glass pane, leaving her handprint behind.

Driven by a mix of dread and determination, I raced outside. Kim was off with her father—they were picking up supplies for dinner. I was alone, as I wanted to be. But this little girl...who was she?

I followed a path through the garden that I hadn't noticed before. It was a narrow, winding trail bordered by overgrown hedges and wildflowers that seemed to thrive in the shade of the towering trees. I still felt the strange coldness but I couldn't see the little girl.

As I walked, the sunlight struggled to pierce through the dense canopy overhead. My steps led me to an ancient tree at the heart of the garden, its trunk gnarled and massive, branches stretching out like the arms of a ghostly sentinel. It had thick branches, many of them, actually. I could not imagine how old this tree might be.

Under the tree, the ground was barren, the grass refusing to grow in its oppressive shade. Hanging from its limbs were dolls—old, tattered, faceless and faded dresses swinging silently in the breeze.

A cold shudder ran through me as I approached; the dolls seemed almost to watch me—even though they had no eyes. On closer inspection I could see that although they had no eyes or noses, they did have mouths. Their stitched smiles twisted in silent screams.

As I stood there, a gust of wind stirred the leaves, and a soft, chilling laughter echoed around me, bouncing off the trees and settling like a cold whisper in my ears. The sound was out of place, hauntingly jovial in the quiet, somber setting, sending shivers down my spine.

I could think of nothing to do but run. Run away, as far and fast as possible.

My retreat from the woods was hurried, haunted by the echoes of the child's ghostly giggles.

I know you, May. I see you. I need a mother. Will thee not love me as a mother?

I paused for a moment in my run. "Who are you?" I screamed at the empty air around me.

Elizabeth. My name is Elizabeth.

"I cannot be your mother, Elizabeth. Go away!"

I couldn't shake the feeling that the laughter was mocking me, taunting me as I stumbled back down the path I had come. The dolls continued to swing behind me, their eerie giggles following me as I left.

The dolls are giggling at me? Have I gone mad?

Every shadow seemed to shift as I passed, every rustle of the leaves sounding like whispers. I quickened my pace, nearly running by the time I reached the open lawn, my breath heavy, my heart pounding in my chest.

Glancing back, I saw nothing but the quiet woods, the dolls unseen but I knew they were still hanging there. The laughter had ceased, but the memory of it clung to me, a haunting melody that seemed to penetrate the very air around River Run.

As I walked back to the house, the weight of the house's secrets felt heavier, more oppressive, as if by witnessing the smiling dolls, I had somehow become part of its somber narrative.

Back at home, I was delighted to see the sedan in the driveway. My husband and daughter had returned. Kim kissed me, begged for a peach and I happily gave her one.

"Stay inside, Kim. I think it might rain," I lied as I began unloading the paper bags. At least they weren't plastic bags.

"What are you talking about, May? There's not a cloud in the sky. What's the matter? I know this place is remote and you must miss the city but please give it a chance." I hated Wen's dismissiveness.

"It's not that. I'll tell you but don't say anything to Kim. I don't want to scare her," I warned him. "I found something. I need to show you."

I recounted everything—the eerie path, the ancient tree, the faceless dolls with their stitched smiles, and the chilling laughter of the child who called herself Elizabeth. The child that wanted a mother.

Wen's face remained unreadable, a stoic mask hiding his thoughts. But beneath his calm exterior, I could see the furrow of his brow, the slight tightening of his jaw.

As a piping designer, he believed in logical explanations, in things seen and measured, yet the fear in my voice, the tremor of my hands as I spoke of the dolls, seemed to breach his skepticism.

That and his guilt. I had the strong feeling that he wouldn't even be entertaining this conversation if I didn't have the emotional upper hand. Not that I wanted it. I prayed that I could forget Wen's betrayal. So far, no luck.

"It could just be kids playing a prank, or maybe some old decorations left from... I don't know, some event," Wen offered tentatively, trying to rationalize what I had experienced. "Do you think that's possible?"

"No, Wen. I do not think that is possible. I saw the girl and those dolls, they are hanging in the tree!"

He tapped my hand softly to remind me to keep my voice down. "I believe you." But his words felt hollow, probably even to him. After a moment of silence, he stood up, a determined look settling over his features.

"Let's go back together," he said. "I'll see it for myself, and we can take down those dolls. It's not good for Kim to see such things."

"Should we wait until she's gone? I don't want her to see these things, or that girl."

"When will that be? We're homeschooling her. Hold that thought. I'll set the computer up for her so she can do her survey. That should keep her busy for a few minutes. Sound like a plan?"

I nodded and went to retrieve scissors and one of the paper bags. After a few minutes, Wen returned and I could hear Kim's computer program welcoming her to her online class orientation.

Wen nodded confidently. "I told her to stay there until she completes the survey. It should take her about thirty minutes. That should give us enough time to see this."

See this? He didn't believe me any more than the man on the moon.

I quickly led him through the yard to the hidden path. Sure enough, the dolls were there. Dozens of them, some of them old. Very old. So old they crumbled when I touched them.

Together, we collected the dolls from the tree, I felt a chill watching Wen touch them. As Wen reached up to pull down the first doll, a gust of wind shook the branches, as if protesting against our actions. I couldn't help but shudder, my skin crawling at the sight of each doll he detached—each one's faceless gaze seeming to bore into me.

I glanced around half expecting to see Elizabeth staring at me but she was not there. At least not visible to the naked eye.

Wen cut each doll down, handed them to me, one by one, their fabric cold and damp in my hands. I dropped the disgusting things in the bag. I tried not to think about the way their mouths were stitched into those grotesque smiles.

As I held the dolls, a whisper of air brushed against my neck, a silent echo of the laughter that had haunted me earlier.

"Hurry," I urged Wen, wanting nothing more than to leave this place and its somber watchfulness behind. "We should burn these. Burn them, Wen. They do not belong in the house. Do not let Kim see them."

My husband opened his mouth to answer me but quickly closed it. "Yeah, let's put them in the burn barrel." That's when I noticed that Kim was watching us from the kitchen window and although Wen said nothing, I could see she was not alone.

Elizabeth, the girl from the tree, the ghost that wanted a mother, was behind her and she was reaching for Kim.

With a violent scream, I dropped the bag and ran for the house.

To my shock, when we made it back inside, Kim was at the kitchen table, talking to her teacher. She'd never been by the window and when I asked her about it, she looked at me like I was old and confused. I was neither.

But now, I knew, we were not alone in this house. Not at all.

Chapter Four–Kim

I was playing in my room, the sunlight peeking through the curtains making patterns on the floor. My toys were scattered around, and I was building a castle with my blocks when my hand brushed against something rough under the bed.

Curious, I lay down on my tummy and pulled the floral bed skirt aside. There, tucked in the dark, hidden corner under my bed, were these weird little dolls. They looked old, made of corn cobs with faces that weren't quite right, they had no eyes but weird stitched smiles that seemed to grin at me.

I didn't remember putting these dolls under there—I don't like dolls much anyway. These ones gave me a funny feeling, like when you think someone is watching you but you can't see anyone. I didn't like that creepy crawly feeling. In fact, I wanted to crawl away, but I couldn't stop looking at them. The old dolls were so strange, like they didn't belong in my sunny room but had come from somewhere dark and strange.

Even though those dolls made me feel all shivery, part of me was curious about them. They weren't like any toys I had ever seen; they seemed like they had their own secrets. I slowly reached out and touched one.

I instantly regretted it. Its body was scratchy, and the stitches on its smile felt all bumpy under my fingers. I wondered who made them and why they looked so weirdly mean.

I pushed them back under the bed because I didn't want to see them anymore.

But even after I scooted back and sat up, I kept thinking about them. There was something about those dolls that didn't let go of my mind. They were creepy, sure, but also sort of fascinating in a way I couldn't understand.

I tried to shake off the goosebumps and focus on my coloring book, hoping that the bright colors would wash away the gray feeling those dolls left in my heart. I loved the Happy Harpy Anime books. They were my favorite.

I flipped open my Happy Harpy Anime coloring book, the one with all the bright, cheerful characters that usually made me smile. I picked up my biggest, brightest pink crayon and started coloring Harpy's wings, trying hard to think about her adventures instead of those creepy dolls. Harpy was always so brave, flying high above the clouds and saving her friends from trouble.

As I filled in the colors, making Harpy's world come alive on the paper, I listened to the normal sounds of our house. I heard Mom humming in the kitchen and the soft thud of Dad's book as he probably dropped it onto the couch again. Those sounds made me feel a bit safer, a bit more grounded in my sunny room.

But just as I was starting to relax, a soft giggle floated up from under the bed. It was light and airy, like it wasn't quite real. I froze, my crayon stopping mid-air. The giggle sounded playful, but in the quiet of my room, it seemed out of place and scary.

My heart started to beat faster, and I felt my grip tighten around the purple crayon. If I wasn't careful, I was going to break this one too. I didn't want to look under the bed, but I knew I had to find out if those dolls were still there, staring at me with their blank eyes with their stitched, grinning smiles.

Taking a deep breath, I slowly lowered the crayon onto my coloring book, trying to make as little noise as possible. I leaned a little closer to the floor, my eyes not quite ready to look under the bed yet.

The giggling continued, a soft, tinkling sound that seemed to bounce lightly from one corner of the room to another. I squeezed my eyes shut for a moment, wishing the noise would just go away. But when I opened them again, I knew I had to face whatever was under there.

With another deep breath, I gently pushed myself off the bed and crept towards the edge, my heart thumping loudly in my chest. I crouched down, my hands shaky as I slowly lifted the floral bed skirt.

The darkness under the bed seemed deeper than before, like a thick, velvety curtain hiding secrets. I squinted, trying to make out shapes in the gloom. There they were—the dolls, still scattered where I had left them, their stitched smiles more menacing now in the dim light.

As I stared, trying to gather the courage to reach in and grab them, a face appeared among the dolls.

It was a ghostly girl, her eyes hollow and her smile too wide. She looked at me, and I felt a cold shiver run down my spine. At that moment, I knew her name, even though her lips did not move. I could hear her voice in my head.

I am Elizabeth. What is your name?

"Kim," I blurted out but her presence was so sudden and so frightening, I couldn't scream—I could only gasp. "My name is Kim."

Do you love my dolls? Can you guess which one is yours? I made one for you.

Her strange giggles filled the room again, louder this time, echoing against the walls. I stumbled backward, my little heart racing as I scrambled away from the bed.

Kim, where are you going? Come play with me!

Scrambling to my feet, I ran as fast as I could to the door of my room. My little legs felt wobbly, but I pushed myself to move faster, desperate to get away from the ghostly girl and her creepy dolls. The hallway light seemed miles away as I burst through the door, almost tripping over the carpet.

I collided into Mom right outside my room.

"Whoa, baby!" Her arms wrapped around me instantly, pulling me close. "What's wrong, Kim?" she asked, her voice filled with worry.

I was panting hard, my words jumbled as I pointed back to my room.

"Under the bed... the girl... Elizabeth!" I managed to say between breaths. Mom looked at me, her eyes wide with confusion and concern. She knelt down to my level, her hands on my shoulders, trying to calm me.

"Elizabeth?" Mom's face turned paler than a sheet of paper. "Okay, I'll check it out, don't you worry," she said softly, giving me a reassuring hug before she stepped towards my room to investigate the strange occurrence.

Mom stepped cautiously into my room, her eyes scanning the shadows. She slowly approached my bed, the same way I had, and gently lifted the floral bed skirt. I watched from the doorway, clutching the frame.

Her gasp was soft but sharp. There they were—the dolls, scattered just as I'd seen them, their eerie smiles stitched in crooked lines. Mom's face went even paler.

"How did you get these? I told your father to get rid of them," she muttered mostly to herself but loud enough for me to hear. She gathered the dolls with a sort of determined grimness, her hands shaking slightly. I wasn't sure how to answer her.

Holding the dolls, Mom turned to look at me, her expression a mix of confusion and deep worry.

"Kim, these don't belong in the house. Next time, don't dig things out of the trash. Hand me that tote bag," she instructed in a sharp tone. I didn't want to give her the rainbow tote bag, it was my favorite one but I wasn't stupid enough to disobey her.

"I didn't dig them out of the trash, Mom. I swear!"

Mom stuffed the dolls in the tote and plopped it on my desk, keeping her distance as if they might jump up and out at any minute.

"You said you saw a girl too, right? Under the bed?" Her voice was steady but I could tell she was scared too. She knelt beside me again, her eyes searching mine for the truth. "Tell me the truth, Kimmie. Did you hear me and your dad talking? What girl are you talking about? What did she look like?"

"Elizabeth talks to me in my head. She has gray skin and she has blonde hair. She wears an old dress, a long one and she has long fingernails. Her name is Elizabeth," I explained, feeling a little braver with Mom so close.

Mom nodded slowly, squeezing my hand. "I believe you but I need you to do me a favor. Next time she talks to you, tell her to go away and tell me. Make sure you tell me. You aren't in trouble. You haven't done anything wrong." She hugged me and I hugged her back. I could feel the tears sting my eyes but I was determined to be brave.

For me and Mom.

"We will figure this out, sweetheart. We'll figure it out together," she reassured me, her voice firm yet gentle.

Mom gripped the tote tightly as she led me down the stairs to the backyard. "We're going to make sure they're gone for good this time," she said with a determination that almost hid her fear. I clutched her hand, looking up at her as we walked.

"But Mom, Elizabeth said one of the dolls was made for me," I whispered, my voice quivering.

Tears blurred my vision, but I tried to be strong like Mom.

She paused, looking down at me with a deep frown. "Which one, Kim?" she asked, her voice gentle. She dumped the tote out on the table, and we searched the stack.

I pointed to the doll with black hair and the horrible, stitched smile that looked too much like a grimace. Mom's expression hardened as she picked it up, examining it closely. It seemed newer, not brittle like the others but just as sinister.

She nodded, understanding flashing in her eyes. "Okay, we'll keep this one out, just to be sure." She stuffed the rest back into the tote and handed me the black-haired doll. "Hold on to this for a moment, sweetheart. We need to do this right."

We reached the burn barrel, and Mom dumped the other dolls inside it. She didn't burn my rainbow bag, thankfully. Instead, she tucked it under her arm.

I watched, clutching the black-haired doll, feeling its yarn hair and the rough stitches under my fingers. *Should I throw it in the barrel too?*

Mom took a deep breath, struck a match, and tossed it into the barrel. The fire caught quickly, the flames licking up and consuming the dolls.

As the flames surged higher, casting eerie shadows on the grass, the whispering grew louder. *Thee hath invoked my wrath!* Elizabeth's voice hissed from the depths of the fire, her words twisted in archaic bends of a long-forgotten English. The black-haired doll in my hands seemed to tremble, its stitched eyes gazing into the inferno.

Thou art cursed, child of the darkness you have become!

"Mom? Can you hear her?" Kim asked me in Korean. The fire crackled in sync with each syllable.

Thy lineage shall know my fury, as thee hath burnt the visages of servants in thine arrogance.

"Mom?"

She shook her head as if she heard nothing at all. But I knew better.

The air grew thick, heavy with the scent of burning cloth and the old, musty smell of secrets long buried. I tried to speak, to ask her to stop, but my voice was lost in the sounds of the crackling wood and the unsettling whispers.

Mom stood beside me, her face pale, her eyes wide with fear.

"Elizabeth, please," I managed to stammer in broken English, my plea mingling with the smoke that rose towards the starless sky. "Shut up! Don't speak to me anymore!"

The doll's mouth moved slightly, as if it were about to speak. Why was I holding this thing? "Burn it, Mom! Burn this one too!" Hot tears streamed down my face.

Thy pleas shall not sway me, for thou hast sealed thine own doom.

Elizabeth's voice echoed around us, chilling and relentless. The ground beneath our feet seemed to pulse with an ancient anger, and the night air turned cold, wrapping its icy fingers around us.

Without waiting for her approval, I tossed the doll into the barrel. She was already threatening me and I was afraid of her.

"Stay close, Kim. Your father will be here soon."

We should have never burned the dolls.

Now, the whispering wouldn't stop. Elizabeth's curses were upon me, threading through generations with a promise of vengeance from beyond the grave.

As the fire crackled, a horrible scream echoed from the house, making both of us jump. It was a wail of anger and despair, not human, chilling to the bone.

Mom turned to me, her face pale but resolute. "It's going to be okay, Kim. I'm going to protect you," she assured me, pulling me into a hug.

I nodded, hoping she could do just that. We watched together as the doll, the one that looked like me, caught fire, the black yarn melting into a twisted smile. It burned to a crisp.

Mom held my hand tightly as we watched the flames dance.

I felt scared but safe next to her, knowing that whatever was trying to scare us, we wouldn't face it alone. Suddenly, I felt a sweet wind, a soft whisper.

It was Goldie. She didn't speak and I am sure Mom did not know she was there but I did.

And that made all the difference.

Chapter Five—Wen

I arrived home with my arms laden with bags of groceries and a bouquet of bright flowers that I had picked up for May to plant in the garden. My wife had a green thumb, she could grow anything. I hoped she would appreciate the gesture.

The scent of fresh earth and vivid flowers; this a small gesture another in my ongoing attempt to mend the rift between us. As I stepped through the front door, the comforting image I had imagined dissipated abruptly. There, in the living room, sat May and our daughter, Kim, their expressions etched with a mix of fear and urgency.

"May, what's going on? Why do you both look like you've seen a ghost?" I asked, setting down the groceries with a thud on the dining room table. The thud echoed slightly in the tense air.

May took a deep breath, her eyes avoiding mine as she spoke. "We had to burn them, Wen. The dolls... they were under Kim's bed. You were supposed to burn them." Her voice was steady, but there was a tremble in her hands that didn't escape my notice.

I froze, processing her words. "Burn the dolls? Of course I did. Why were they under Kim's bed? Did you put them there, Kimmy?" The questions tumbled out, each one laced with confusion and disbelief.

"No, Daddy!" Kim's voice was shrill, her small face crumpled with frustration. "I didn't put them there, I swear. I have never even seen them before. But I heard her, the ghost—she talks to me." Her confession sent a cold shiver down my spine, the hairs on my neck standing on end. "In here," she pointed at her temple.

I turned to May, searching her face for an explanation, hoping she had influenced Kim's tale in some way. "You told her about the ghost?" I accused her, the words sharper than I had intended. "You don't even know if it was a ghost."

"No, Wen! I didn't tell her anything. She told me! She hears her voice in her head, and I believe her," May snapped back, her patience fraying. I could see in her eyes that she was as bewildered and scared as I was, maybe more.

With a heavy sigh, I walked back outside to the barrel where the dolls had been burned.

A cloud of smoke still lingered, the smell of charred fabric hanging heavily in the air. Sifting through the ashes with a long stick, I uncovered the remnants of the dolls. They had all burned to cinders, all except one.

It lay there, half-burned, its features eerily resembling Kim's. I wanted to vomit. What did this mean?

My heart pounded against my chest as I quickly covered up the doll again, deciding in that moment to keep this disturbing discovery to myself. Back inside, the tension had only grown. Kim hugged my neck and went to the kitchen with a bag in her hand. "I'll put the groceries away."

I reached out to May, my hand hovering in the space between us. "What really happened," I asked softly. "You can tell me."

She recoiled as if my touch burned her. "What really happened? What do you want, Wen?" Her eyes narrowed angrily and she offered no comfort.

"I want to help. I want to protect my family, of course."

To my surprise, she laughed. It was an ugly sound. "Like you helped by cheating on me with that bitch?" Her words were laced with a bitterness that stung deeply.

"May, you have to forgive me at some point," I pleaded, the desperation in my voice clear.

"You'd like that, wouldn't you? You'd move that bitch in here, with my daughter. That will never happen! Over my dead body!" she hissed.

Her anger was a palpable force, and I stumbled over my words in haste. "She's not a bitch, her name is Carly. It's not like you to talk like that. It meant nothing. Nothing at all," I blurted out, immediately regretting it as her frown deepened.

"And that helps?" she shot back coldly. "You stick a part of your body inside another woman's body and that's nothing? Hey, why don't I run out and do that too? Since we're just sleeping with whomever nowadays.

The battle went on. We did our best to keep the argument to a dull roar, but Kim heard us. I knew that. She put the groceries up and went upstairs to leave her parents to fight.

We went to bed that night with the chasm between us wider than ever, Kim asleep between us, a small barrier in an ever-growing divide.

Desperation clawed at me as the dawn crept through the curtains of our troubled home.

The chill of the morning matched the coldness settling in my heart from the night's harsh words with May. I couldn't shake the eerie whispers that had seeped into our lives, or the unsettling image of the unburned doll that resembled Kim.

In a bid to find some resolution, or at least an understanding, I decided to reach out to the previous owners of River Run, the Boysons, whose hasty departure now seemed ominously prescient. I'd have to tell May about it but afterward, of course. It was easier to get forgiveness than permission.

Pacing the dew-kissed grass of our backyard, I dialed the realtor with shaky hands, my breath forming small clouds in the crisp air. After a few terse exchanges and promises of confidentiality, I was given a number that I dialed without hesitation. Each ring echoed like a distant drum in the fog, my heart syncing with its rhythm.

"Sophia Boyson speaking," came the hesitant voice, as if emerging from the shadows of a haunted past.

"Sophia, this is Wen... Wen Lee. We bought River Run from you," I started, my voice steadier than I felt.

There was a pause, a breath held in a collective memory of fear. "Mr. Lee, I hoped I'd never hear that name again," Sophia's voice trembled slightly, revealing cracks in her composed facade.

"I--I apologize for bringing it up. But I need your help—we need your help. Strange things are happening--things involving our daughter, Kim," I confessed, the morning sun doing little to warm the chill that settled deeper in my bones. "She's only five, Mrs. Boyson. Please, help me. I just have a few questions."

Another silence followed; this one heavy with unspoken dread. "I feared as much," Sophia finally replied, her tone resigned. "It seems the house never really lets go of anyone."

I urged her to meet us, to share what they knew, to help us understand what was targeting Kim. The desperation in my plea must have reached through the phone because after a long, heavy pause, she agreed.

"We'll meet you at the coffee shop by the old mill. Tomorrow morning. Nine o'clock," she said, her voice a mix of reluctance and resolve.

"Thank you, Mrs. Boyson. Thank you so much."

Hanging up, I felt a flicker of hope, a thin wisp of smoke in the dense fog of our fears. Tomorrow, I thought, might just shed light on the dark corners of River Run.

As my family and I approached the coffee shop the next morning, the old mill's weathered facade loomed in the background like a silent guardian of past secrets.

The crisp autumn air nipped at my skin as I crossed the parking lot, my thoughts racing. I rehearsed the questions I wanted to ask the

Boysons, each one a stepping stone towards understanding or, perhaps, a path to a deeper abyss.

Mike and Sophia Boyson were already there, sitting at a table outside. They looked older than the last time I had seen them, weariness etched into their features, a stark reminder of the toll River Run might have exacted on them too. Still, they were an attractive couple. As I approached, they rose to greet us, their expressions a complex mix of apprehension and muted politeness.

"Mr. Lee," Mike extended his hand first, his grip firm yet somehow tentative. "Mike Boyson. Good to see you."

"Thank you for meeting us," I nodded to Kim as we sat down. She looked at me with her soft brown eyes and I naturally said yes. May wanted to keep her close but the playground was a part of the coffee shop's property. It's not like I couldn't see her.

"Stay close," May added as Kim ran for the swings. There were other children already playing and other parents sipping on their favorite coffees.

The initial awkwardness hung between us like an impenetrable mist. I cleared my throat, grateful for the steaming cup of coffee the server placed in front of me.

"Thank you for meeting us on such short notice," I began, watching their faces for any signs of regret or reluctance. "I wouldn't have reached out if it weren't serious. Our daughter, Kim—she's experiencing things... seeing things. My wife May and I are concerned. At first, it seemed harmless enough but it's gotten worse."

Sophia interlaced her fingers tightly in front of her. "We understand, Mr. Lee. We had hoped the house's... history wouldn't repeat itself. But it seems it has a hold on whoever lives there."

Mike nodded, his eyes dark under the brim of his cap. "When we lived there, our middle child--our only girl, Evie, she... she started acting strangely. Heard voices, saw shadows moving. We all did. Mary Sanford was truly a witch, I don't care what people say. Is that who you're seeing in the house?"

May's eyes widened. "No. We haven't seen Mary Sanford, only Elizabeth. She is the one talking to Kim. She says she hears her in her head." Their words were like cold fingers down my spine.

I glanced at May who seemed as if she were somewhere else mentally but then I realized she was keeping her attention focused on Kim.

Sophia hesitated, then sighed. "Mary Sanford is at rest, as far as we know. We had help, two psychics in the area helped us. But Elizabeth

Kelly...are you sure it's a little girl? Not something posing as a child?"

"How can we tell?" I pressed, eager for any detail that might help protect Kim.

"I'm not sure" Mike interjected, his voice low. "We did our best to cleanse the place, twice but after everything that happened, we couldn't take it anymore. The atmosphere... it was oppressive, always feeling like someone was watching us. The realtor didn't tell you about any of this?"

May and I both shook our heads. The four of us watched Kim play with the other children.

A silence fell as we all considered her words. I felt a chill despite the morning sun warming my back. The casual play of light and shadows around us suddenly seemed sinister, as if hinting at unseen watchers just beyond our perception.

"Mrs. Boyson, you mentioned the house having a history. Do you know anything specific? Anything at all that might help?" I asked, desperate for any piece of information.

Sophia and Mike exchanged a glance, a silent conversation passing between them. "There were stories," Sophia finally said. "Old stories about the original owners. Apparently the original builder, Judge Sanford, was an unholy man. He made deals with the devil, or so they say. His son and daughter-in-law got caught up in it. But then there were also the Kellys and the Ayres. Some tragedy, an accident where a young girl died. They say Elizabeth never left River Run. I never understood how she ended up there to begin with. If Goody Ayres was treating her, why would Elizabeth's spirit show up at River Run?"

May sighed audibly and I put my hand on her shoulder briefly before she flinched. I quickly removed it.

Mike placed his hand over Sophia's. "We didn't believe it until we lived it," he said softly. "And now, unfortunately, it seems you are living it too."

As we continued to talk, Kim played on the outdoor playground, her laughter a stark contrast to our grave discussion. The irony wasn't lost on me; the innocence of youth shadowed by the specters of the past.

The Boysons promised to share more details and to help however they could. As they stood to leave, Sophia leaned in, her voice a whisper. "Be careful, Mr. Lee. That house, it's more than just wood and stone. It remembers. And it seems to have a purpose we don't fully understand."

With their words echoing in my mind, I watched them go, feeling the weight of our haunted dwelling more profoundly than ever.

Tomorrow might bring some light, but today, it seemed the shadows held sway.

Chapter Six–Sophia

At home, in the dim light of the evening, Mike and I sat at our old oak kitchen table, a spread of yellowed papers and old books laid out between us. The topic of Elizabeth Kelly had resurfaced—a tale so steeped in local legend and whispers that we'd almost forgotten it amid our own ordeals.

"I never really believed it," I admitted, flipping through a book on the area's history. "All those stories about Elizabeth being a witch, cursed from birth... It seemed like just another ghost story, meant to scare children."

Mike rubbed his temples, weary from the discussion. "Yeah, it was easier to dismiss it as a myth. But after everything that happened, can we really say it was all just stories?" He looked at me, his eyes searching for some hint of agreement or perhaps reassurance.

What was I supposed to say? I didn't suppose this was a good time to tell him that I was pregnant again although I originally planned to this weekend. Nope. That will have to wait. I'll tell him after.

The silence that followed was heavy, filled with the echoes of our past fears and the undeniable reality of our experiences at River Run.

"I'm going to get a shower. Make sure the kids are in bed. I don't want them to see all this," Mike kissed my forehead.

"Yeah, you're probably right. Thanks, honey."

As night deepened, I couldn't pull myself away from the research. Boxes of files and notes, once packed away in the hope of never needing them again, were now strewn across the living room floor.

Each document whispered fragments of Elizabeth's story, but nothing concrete, nothing that felt like truth. Just strange accounts of Millie Ayres, the daughter of Goody witnessing Elizabeth making the silverware levitate once or twice. Other weird things too, like the time little Elizabeth Kelly made the flower sing and once choked another girl almost to death without even touching her.

Mike came back downstairs, a frown creasing his brow as he saw me surrounded by the chaos of our haunted past. "Sophia, maybe we should just let the Lee family handle it. Like we did. We could introduce them to Sabrina. She'll know what to do."

I looked up at him, a sharp retort ready on my lips. But then I saw the concern in his eyes, the genuine fear for our family's peace, and softened. "You don't really mean that, do you?" I asked, though the answer was clear in his hesitation.

"You're telling me you don't feel bad at all? Your heart doesn't go out to them?"

He sighed, the weight of unspoken guilt in his gaze. "Yes, my heart breaks for them but I don't want to put you or the kids in harm's way again," he confessed quietly.

The truth was, neither of us could just walk away, not when another family was threading through the same dark labyrinth we had barely escaped. Our silence, our decisions, they all had weights and consequences, tied as tightly to us as the history of River Run itself.

The next morning, I was standing in front of the bathroom mirror, applying the last touches of mascara, trying to ready myself for another day at work.

Ugh. Time for new mascara. This mascara was old and full of clumps.

My thoughts were still swirling with the remnants of last night's conversation lingering in my mind. The sound of small, hesitant steps approached, and then the bathroom door creaked open. I didn't even have to look. It was my mini me.

Evie, her curls tousled from sleep, clutched her new pink teddy bear close as she peeked inside. Her big eyes met mine in the mirror, a curious mix of innocence and something tinged with an old, weary concern that shouldn't be present in a seven-year-old's gaze.

"Want some mascara?" I offered with a smile. She smiled and closed her eyes. Naturally, she blinked several times, making a mess. We both laughed as I cleaned her face.

"Mommy, why were you talking about River Run last night? And about Elizabeth?" she asked, her voice small and worried. The mention of Elizabeth Kelly's name coming from Evie's lips sent a chill through me.

I turned to face her, crouching down to her level. "Sweetie, why are you asking about that now? Has someone mentioned her to you? What have I told you about eavesdropping?" The possibility that the stories had somehow reached her filled me with a sudden dread.

Evie shook her head, her curls bouncing slightly. "No, ma'am. I haven't been eavesdropping but sometimes I hear her. She calls me Witch Child, but I tell her that's not my name. My name is Evelyn Heart Boyson." Her words were so matter-of-fact, yet the underlying fear was palpable. At least to me.

All this time and I'd never known that she'd followed us here.

A cold knot formed in my stomach. "She calls you?" I managed to say, keeping my voice steady despite the panic rising within me. I closed the mirror and zipped the cosmetic bag before tossing it in the drawer.

"Yes," Evie continued, looking up at me with those deep, trusting eyes. "She calls me Witch Child, but when I tell her she's wrong, she goes away. Other times, she just stares at me from the yard, but she can't come in here. Not in the new house. She can't come in because she doesn't like the horseshoe."

"The horseshoe?" I asked, forgetting momentarily that Sabrina had suggested they nail the iron horseshoe above the door. Iron, especially old iron, like the horseshoe was a witch repellent.

I pulled her into a tight hug, my heart pounding with a mix of fear and anger. That Elizabeth's presence could reach out to us still, despite all the distances and barriers we'd put up, was a thought I couldn't bear.

"Mommy, you can't go back there, okay? River Run is far away, and you're safe here with us and Daddy."

I reassured her, stroking her hair to soothe us both. "But what about the other girl? I don't want to go back there but there's another family. "

Evie whispered into my shoulder, her voice muffled. "Her name is Kim. Elizabeth wants her to be the next Witch Child."

The statement rocked me back on my heels. I held her, frozen, unsure what to do. That Evie could know such specifics chilled me to the bone. "It's okay, love," I murmured, choosing my words carefully. "We're going to make sure that doesn't happen. You're safe, and we'll keep her safe too."

Evie nodded, seeming to accept this assurance, her grip on me loosening a little. As she skipped out of the bathroom, the weight of her words lingered, settling around me like a cold mist.

How much did she understand? And how much were we, as her parents, failing to protect her from forces we barely comprehended ourselves? The need to act, to do something—anything—to shield not just our family but the Lees as well, became a burning imperative in my heart.

Later that day, after Evie had gone to school and the house had quieted, I sat in our small study, a space filled with books and mementos of a life before River Run.

My hands trembled slightly as I picked up the phone to call Mike. The morning's revelations from Evie were haunting me, and I needed to share these fears with him. I knew he was at work but I needed to hear his voice.

As soon as he answered, I could hear the familiar bustling sounds of his office in the background. "Mike, got a minute?"

"For you, of course. Everything okay?"

"Yes, I think so, but I had an interesting conversation with Evie this morning," I started, my voice low. There was a pause, and then a quiet acknowledgment.

"I've been thinking about it since you texted. It's... it's unsettling, Sophia. How did she know about Kim?"

I whispered, clutching the phone tighter. "She did mention Kim, Lee's daughter. She said Elizabeth wants her to be the next Witch Child. How could she know that unless it's true? What if Elizabeth is still reaching out from that place? What if she really was an evil child? I can't believe that a child, even a dead child, would stalk other children."

Mike's sigh was heavy, laden with a tiredness that spoke of too many battles fought. "I've been skeptical, Sophia, about all those stories. But now, with Evie saying these things...what Kim is experiencing. It's hard to dismiss."

"Skepticism doesn't seem like a luxury we can afford anymore," I said, a cold draft seeming to sweep through the room as I spoke. "The mediums, the stories about Mary Sanford's dealings... It's all converging. And now, Evie's involved somehow again."

There was a silence as we both absorbed the weight of the situation. Mike then spoke, his voice firmer. "We can't ignore this. I'll come home early today. We should go over everything again, see if there's anything we missed that could help the Lees... and Evie."

That evening, as I waited for Mike, I leaned against him on our porch swing, the autumn air crisp around us. Our conversation turned to the realtor, Carmen, who had sold us River Run, and the guilt of having walked into that nightmare, unknowing and unprepared.

"I don't want to go back, Mike, but we let them walk in there," I murmured, tears welling up. "Carmen—she should have told them. It was her responsibility too."

Mike wrapped an arm around me, pulling me close. "We'll help the Lees, Sophia. We have to. I won't let what happened to us happen to them."

I nodded, feeling the resolve built within us. "I'll call Aunt Pat. She can come stay with the kids." My voice was more confident now, bolstered by the need to protect not just my own family but another from the shadows that had so deeply touched our lives.

As the night drew in, the resolve that had been forged between us felt like a beacon in the darkness.

We were no longer isolated in our fears; we were a team, ready to delve deeper into the mysteries of River Run, ready to face whatever truths lay hidden in its shadows. The decision was made.

We would help, no matter the cost.

Hopefully, it wouldn't cost us everything.

Chapter Seven–Kim

In the quiet darkness of my room, the shadows seemed to twist and stir as I struggled against the tangles of my blanket. I hated sleeping in this house. I hated River Run. I wish we could leave and never come back.

My sleep was no longer a peaceful escape; instead, it had become a doorway to a scary place that felt too real to be just a dream.

I heard whispers, soft and sweet, like the wind rustling through the leaves outside my window, but these weren't friendly. They invited me to step into the woods behind our house.

"Come, Kim," they called, and I felt my heart beat faster with both excitement and fear. I both wanted to go and didn't want to go but this was a dream. Anything was possible in a dream. Right? "Come play with us!"

The voice in my dream told me to follow the red rose petals scattered on the ground. Where had they come from? Mom had roses but none of them were red.

They shimmered under the moonlight, leading deeper into the woods. "Follow them, Kim. They will lead you to a prize," the whisper promised. I didn't know what prize awaited, but the petals looked so pretty, like the trail to a fairy tale treasure.

As I walked in my dream, the forest around me didn't look like the one I played in during the day. It was darker, stranger, with trees that twisted into weird shapes and shadows that moved on their own.

The air felt colder too, and I hugged myself, wishing I had my big fluffy jacket. But the red petals on the ground kept leading me on, a bright contrast to the dark earth, and I couldn't stop myself from following them.

I wanted to see where they led, even though I was really, really scared.

The red petals led me deeper and deeper, and the trees grew taller and their branches thicker, like they were trying to block out the moonlight.

I kept following the petals because I wanted to see the prize, but I was starting to feel like maybe this wasn't such a good idea. The whispers grew louder, no longer just a gentle coaxing but urgent, pushing me to hurry.

But this is a dream. Just a dream.

Suddenly, Elizabeth appeared. She was older than me and looked strange, like she wasn't from now but a long time ago. Her clothes were old-fashioned, like the ones in the big picture book of pioneers.

Elizabeth's hair was long and shiny, and her eyes were sad but kind of scary too. She didn't look dead in my dream. She looked like a real girl. A real girl who was my real friend.

"This way, Kim," she said, her voice like the whispering wind. I followed her into what looked like a really scary version of the woods behind River Run.

Everything was twisted—the trees bent in impossible ways, and the air was filled with a thick fog that made it hard to see. The red petals continued along a narrow path that led to an even darker part of the forest.

I didn't want to go there, but my feet moved on their own, like I was in one of those puppet shows where the puppets don't get to decide what they do. *Not a puppet. Not a Muppet. But a marionette. I learned that recently. Marionette. It was a weird word for sure.*

As I walked following behind Elizabeth, the ground became mushy under my feet, squishing with every step. It was really icky, and I tried not to think about what I was stepping in. My bunny slippers were going to be ruined.

That's when I saw them—the hands. They started coming out of the ground, reaching for me. Reaching for my slippers. The hands were pale and looked like they wanted to grab me and pull me down. I screamed and ran, the cold fingers just missing my feet.

I looked ahead to see if Elizabeth was still there, and she was, but she didn't seem scared at all. She saw the hands and she smiled. She just kept calling me, telling me to hurry, to come to her.

But I didn't want to go to her anymore.

I wanted to go home. I wanted Mom and Dad. I wanted to wake up. But the dream wouldn't let me. I kept running through the creepy woods, away from the hands, following the red petals that seemed to go on forever.

Finally, after what seemed like forever running through the twisted woods, the path opened up into a small clearing. The trees pulled back as if making room for what lay in the center.

My breath caught in my throat when I saw it— the same tree from my backyard at River Run, but it wasn't just any tree now. It looked menacing, larger, with its branches hanging low, heavy with shadows. It was like some sort of monster, but a tree monster.

Hanging from the branches, like some horrible decorations, were dolls. Dolls with no faces. They swayed gently in the breeze, they had no eyes. Just weird smiles and frowns.

And there, among them, was a doll that looked just like me. I remembered seeing it burn in the fire, so how could it be here? I felt tears pricking my eyes as fear gripped me tighter.

Elizabeth stood beneath the tree, her expression serious. "See, Kim? They're not gone. They can never really be gone," she said, her voice echoing around the clearing. "I was once a Witch Child, just like you could be. I could do many things, and so can you. Don't you want to be strong? So strong that no one can ever hurt you?"

Her words confused and scared me. "Nobody hurts me. I'm not a witch," I stuttered, stepping back. "I don't want to be a witch."

"But you are, naturally," Elizabeth insisted, stepping closer. Her face was still kind, but her eyes were intense, almost glowing. "You have powers, Kim. You can make things happen just like I did. I can make flowers laugh and bring dead birds back to life. I can curse the cruel and make those that hate me pay. Don't you want to learn how?"

"Why aren't you talking strange? You seem different," I shook my head, my heart pounding so loud I could hear it in my ears. "I want to go home," I whispered, looking around for a way out.

Elizabeth frowned angrily, then suddenly smiled. "Thee should try to wake then," she challenged. "I will be myself with thee, Kim, Witch Child."

I remembered what my grandma had once told me about bad dreams. "If you ever feel stuck, pinch yourself, and you'll wake up." So, I pinched my arm hard, hoping to feel the pain and snap out of the dream. But nothing happened. I pinched harder, tears now streaming down my face.

"Wake up, Kim, wake up!" I cried out to myself.

Just as I started to feel hopeless, a tall, handsome man appeared next to Elizabeth. He squatted down to my level, his smile warm but his eyes cold. He put his arm around Elizabeth's waist.

"I see you've met my daughter. Come here, Kim. Don't be afraid. We're your friends," he coaxed, stretching out his hand towards me. "We can even be family. Again."

I almost stepped forward, drawn by his calming presence, but then I remembered Elizabeth's unsettling smile at the hands that stole my bunny slippers.

Just then, a loud, fierce scream filled the air, breaking the spell. It was Goldie, my favorite cartoon ghost, floating next to me, her face twisted in anger.

"No, Kim! Don't listen to them!" Goldie yelled in Korean. I blinked, and for a second, I saw the man's face change, his smile twisting into something mean and scary. He rose to his fate and ran toward my grandmother and me.

I screamed, the sound loud and desperate, echoing through the woods, trying to break free from the nightmare that held me tight.

My scream tore through the night, a sharp, jarring cry that seemed to shatter the eerie silence of River Run. In my room, the shadows that had played on the walls now seemed to recoil, as if startled by the sound of my fear.

Mom and Dad burst into the room, flicking on the light and rushing to my side. The sudden brightness made me squint, but it was a relief to see their worried faces rather than the haunting images from my dream.

"Daddy! Mommy!" I cried out, throwing my arms around them. The memory of the dream was still too real, too frightening. I buried my face in Dad's shirt, trying to forget the cold, dark eyes of the man and Elizabeth's twisted smile.

"Sweetheart, it's okay, you're safe. It was just a bad dream," Mom soothed, stroking my hair as she sat on the edge of my bed. Her voice was calm, but I could feel her heart racing as she held me close.

"But it was so real!" I sobbed. "The man and Elizabeth, they wanted to take me! And my doll, it was hanging from the tree even though it burned! And Goldie saved me!" The words tumbled out in a rush, each one laced with the raw fear I had felt.

Dad looked at Mom, his face lined with concern. "It's okay, Kim. We're here now. Nobody is going to take you," he assured me, but his glance at Mom told me he was as scared as I was by what I had said. "It was just a dream."

"No! They took my bunny slippers! Look! They're gone, Dad! Look! Just look!" I was crying so hard I could hardly believe it. I glanced beside my bed and could see that the slippers were gone. I'd already known that. "I don't want to be a Witch Child! Please! Go away!"

We spent the rest of the night together in my room, with Mom and Dad taking turns to hold me until I fell asleep again.

The nightmare had shaken us all, and even though they tried to hide it, I could tell Mom and Dad were worried. This wasn't just any nightmare; it was something more, something darker that lingered in the air like the cold touch of a shadow.

In the light of day, recounting the dream made it feel somewhat less terrifying, but the echoes of that fear remained, a cold undercurrent in the sunny morning.

As I spoke, the adults exchanged looks, their faces growing more serious.

I couldn't tell if they were mad at me or if I was in trouble. I needn't have worried. Mom held me close and so did Dad.
No matter what happened, we would always be together. Somehow I knew this and it gave me comfort.

Chapter Eight–May

As the shadows lengthened across the living room, casting eerie patterns on the floor. Why in this house did shadows seem to have a mind of their own? It was so distracting I could barely understand what my husband was saying.

Wen brought up the name Sabrina once more. He had mentioned her before, a psychic known to have some insight into matters of the spiritual realm, the sort of insight that made my skin crawl just thinking about it. She came highly recommended by the Boysons.

"Sabrina could help us understand what's happening, May. She could help protect Kim," Wen urged, his eyes earnest, pleading. I could see the desperation there, the raw fear for our daughter, but it clashed violently with the knot of skepticism and fear in my own stomach.

Bringing in a psychic felt like crossing a threshold from which there was no return. To acknowledge that our home, our sanctuary, might be tainted by something otherworldly was a step I wasn't sure I was ready to take. It felt like opening a door to confirm there was a monster lurking on the other side, waiting.

"I don't know, Wen," I hesitated, my voice tight. "This stuff with spirits and psychics... It feels like we might be inviting more trouble. If she's so effective, why is Elizabeth Kelly pursuing our child?" My hands were trembling slightly, a physical manifestation of my internal turmoil.

Wen ran a hand through his hair, frustration lining his face. "May, I understand your fear, I do. But isn't the real trouble already here? Kim's nightmares, the whispers, the doll... We can't just ignore these things. Sabrina comes highly recommended. She's dealt with this kind of situation before and she's familiar with River Run and it's sordid history."

The thought of Kim, so small and terrified, her cries echoing in my ears from her last nightmare, chipped away at my resolve. She was getting worse, not better. Each night seemed to draw more out of her, leaving her paler, quieter. The mother in me battled with the skeptic, with the fear that acknowledging the haunting would somehow make it more real, more powerful.

But Wen was right about one thing—we couldn't ignore it.

Kim's safety was my priority, and if this Sabrina could help dispel whatever was haunting our daughter, then perhaps it was a risk we needed to take.

"Okay," I finally said, the word feeling heavy and foreign on my tongue. "Bring in your psychic. Let's see if she can help our little girl." My voice was resigned, but inside, the storm of doubt and fear raged stronger. "But I mean it. If I say it's over, if I pull the plug..."

"Agreed. We will do this together, May."

What were we inviting into our home? What if this only made things worse? The questions plagued me, but the image of Kim's frightened face pushed me forward. For her, I would face this, whatever it might bring.

The following afternoon, the atmosphere in our home shifted palpably as we awaited Sabrina's arrival. The air felt thick, as if charged with an electric current that buzzed silently through the walls of River Run. Even the usual daylight seemed to struggle against the gloom that had settled over the house, filtering through the curtains with less warmth than it had the day before. I slung the curtains back but it didn't seem to help brighten the place.

Wen paced by the front window, casting anxious glances down the winding driveway, while I tidied up mechanically, my movements sharp and jittery. Every creak of the house, every whisper of wind against the glass, seemed to herald her arrival—or something else, something waiting just beyond our sight.

Finally, a car pulled up—a sleek, black sedan that seemed to absorb the light rather than reflect it. Kim sprang off the couch to look at the stranger that was supposed to help us. I tried to explain all this to her, but she didn't ask too many questions. Five year olds don't question much and believe fantasies far too easily.

Sabrina stepped out, her presence as commanding as the stories suggested. She was a tall woman, draped in a flowing dark shawl that fluttered slightly with the breeze, her hair pulled back tightly, revealing sharp, discerning eyes that seemed to take in more than what was visible.

Wen opened the door before she could knock, his manners overridden by urgency.

"Thank you for coming, Sabrina," he said, his voice a mix of relief and tension. "Sophia and Mike highly recommended you. Thank you for coming on such short notice."

Sabrina nodded, stepping inside with a calm that contrasted starkly with the nervous energy Wen and I carried. "Let's not waste time," she said, her voice resonant and clear. "Wen? You must be May. And you must be Kim. I am so happy to meet you." She extended her hand to each of us and smiled. But then the smile vanished.

"Show me where you sleep. Where you feel the most fear, Kim."

My daughter took her hand and I felt a chill run down my spine. The hallway seemed darker, the portraits on the walls watching us pass.

Kim's room, usually a sanctuary of warmth and childish joy, now felt like the epicenter of an unseen storm. Sabrina paused at the threshold, her eyes closing briefly as if to gather strength—or perhaps information from the air itself.

She stepped inside, her movements deliberate. The room's temperature seemed to drop, causing goosebumps to rise on my arms. Sabrina walked slowly around, touching Kim's small pillows, her toys, lingering by the window where the curtains fluttered slightly.

"I like your room, Kim. It is a very pretty place." She turned her attention to Wen and me, "But there's a strong presence here," she murmured, almost to herself. Turning to us, her expression was serious, her eyes piercing. "I can feel her... the Witch Child. She's very strong, very angry, and very attached to Kim."

Wen gripped my hand, his fingers cold. I tried to speak, to ask what we could do, but the words caught in my throat. What in the world?

Sabrina's gaze met mine, and it was as though she read my unspoken fears. "I will do what I can to protect your daughter and cleanse your home. But you must be prepared. This won't be easy, and it might get worse before it gets better."

The tension in the room escalated, the air now thick with the weight of her words, the promise of a battle against something we could not see but could feel, pressing in around us.

As Sabrina settled into a worn armchair in Kim's room, her shawl draped around her like a cloak of shadows, the atmosphere grew tense with anticipation. Wen and I stood by the doorway, uncertain, as Sabrina began to chant in a low, rhythmic tone that seemed to resonate with the walls of the room itself.

The light dimmed as if the sun outside had been obscured by a sudden cloud. Kim clung to my leg, her small face buried against my jeans, her body tense.
Sabrina's eyes were closed, her hands extended, palms up, as she continued her incantations. A cold breeze filtered through the room, though the windows were shut tight, and the curtains fluttered more violently.

"Spirits of the house," Sabrina intoned, "reveal your intention." Her voice grew louder, more forceful. The toys on Kim's shelves rattled slightly, a picture frame on the wall shook, and a chill swept through the room, causing Kim to whimper in fear.

"Mommy, I'm scared," she whispered, squeezing my hand.

"It's okay, baby," I reassured her in Korean, though my voice trembled, betraying my own fear. I took a step back, with my daughter. We watched from the open doorway.

As Sabrina's chants escalated, a low moaning sound filled the room, like the wind howling through a narrow gap. It grew in intensity, becoming a wail that seemed to come from the very walls of River Run.

I felt my heart pounding, my breaths short and sharp. Wen moved closer, his presence a small comfort.

Suddenly, Sabrina's body stiffened, and her face contorted in concentration. "He's here," she gasped, her voice strained as if she were carrying a great weight. "The One Who Walks Here... he wants this child. He wants your daughter. She's a natural witch!"

"No!" I cried out, the room spinning around me as the implication of her words sank in. "That can't be!"

Sabrina's eyes snapped open, her gaze piercing. "He's been bound here for centuries, a watcher, waiting for one who could see as he saw, feel what he felt. Your daughter, she has the gift, and he knows it. She isn't the first and won't be the last."

The hallway grew colder, and I could see my breath in the air. Shadows seemed to creep closer from the corners of the room, gathering around Sabrina like dark tendrils. She continued, her voice a beacon in the growing darkness.

"He is powerful, and he is angry. We need to protect her, now, before—"

She was cut off as a loud crash echoed through the room. A bookshelf had toppled over, books spilling out like scattered thoughts.

Kim screamed, clinging to me as I scooped her into my arms. Wen rushed to help Sabrina, who seemed to struggle against an unseen force.

Sabrina panted, pushing back against whatever pressed down on her. "This is a curse, deep-seated, woven into the very fabric of this house. I need more help. I must call for my friend, David Ray. He is a powerful medium, a natural witch like your daughter. He may be our only hope."

The promise of further assistance was a thin lifeline thrown into the turbulent seas that our lives had become. As Sabrina gathered herself, steadying her breathing, I held Kim tight, her small body shivering against mine.

We were in the eye of a storm I had never imagined could exist, fighting against shadows that sought to engulf us. The battle for our daughter's soul had just begun.

"Don't stay here tonight. Do you have somewhere else to go?"

I shook my head but the idea of leaving sounded wonderful. "A hotel. There's a hotel about ten miles from here. Wen! We have to pack! Kim! Come with me."

As Wen rushed to gather a few essentials for our unexpected departure, the urgency of Sabrina's warning echoed through my mind, heightening the already palpable tension.

Kim clung to me, her small frame trembling as I grabbed some clothes, her favorite blanket, and the stuffed bunny she couldn't sleep without. Each movement was hurried, frantic with the need to escape the oppressive atmosphere of River Run.

"We need to be quick, May," Wen called out from the bedroom, his voice strained. "Sabrina said it's not safe, especially at night."

I nodded, zipping up Kim's small backpack, the weight of our situation sinking deeper.

How had our life shifted so suddenly into this nightmare? I thought, trying to keep my composure for Kim's sake.

Back in the living room, Sabrina was packing up her things, her expression grave.

"I've contacted David Ray," she informed us, securing the clasp on her leather bag. "He's aware of the situation and is preparing to come here first thing in the morning. But you shouldn't be here when he arrives. It's better to confront him without having to worry about your immediate safety."

Wen and I exchanged worried glances, understanding the gravity of what that confrontation might entail. "Will you be okay here by yourself?" Wen asked, concern etching his features.

Sabrina offered a tight smile, her confidence not quite reaching her eyes. "I've dealt with dangerous entities before. I'll perform a protective ritual and prepare the space for David's arrival. Don't worry about me; just make sure you and your family are safe."

As we loaded our car, the sun began to dip below the horizon, casting long shadows that seemed to stretch ominously across the ground. The air grew cooler, and the sense of something lurking just out of sight grew stronger.

"Mom, will the bad things follow us to the hotel?" Kim's voice was small, filled with fear.

I knelt down, taking her face in my hands. "No, sweetheart, they won't. We're going to a safe place, and Sabrina and her friend will make sure nothing bad can get to us." I hoped my words were more reassuring than I felt.

Wen started the car, the engine's hum a comforting sound against the creeping silence of the evening. As we drove away, I couldn't help but glance back at River Run, its windows dark like hollow eyes watching us leave.

The feeling of being watched didn't subside as we made our way down the twisting drive, and only when we reached the main road did I feel a slight easing of the tension in my shoulders.

The hotel was a bland, unremarkable building beside the highway, but it had never seemed more like a sanctuary. We checked in, and as we settled into our room, the normalcy of the place—its plain walls, the impersonal paintings, the hum of the air conditioner—felt strangely comforting.

That night, we huddled together in our hotel room, the events at River Run seeming both distant and perilously close.

Kim slept fitfully between Wen and me, her small hand gripped tightly in mine. Every creak and sigh of the building kept me awake, alert to any sign of the unnatural.

As the night deepened, I lay there, my thoughts racing. What were we facing? How deep did the curse at River Run go? And could Sabrina and her friend really protect us?

The uncertainty was maddening, but the immediate fear for Kim's safety overshadowed all else.

We were in the eye of a storm, and the coming days promised to test us in ways we'd never imagined.

Morning light would bring David Ray and, with him, hopefully, some answers or a plan.

For now, all we could do was wait, watch, and hold each other close in the long shadows of the night.

Chapter Nine–David Ray

As I hung up the phone after speaking with Sabrina, a sense of foreboding washed over me, tinged with an undercurrent of excitement. I felt it was important that Sophia and Mike Boyson attend too, as they had been involved in this too.

The River Run case wasn't just another haunting—it was steeped in the lore of the Fairfield Witch Trials, a slice of history that I had studied extensively but never expected to confront so directly.

My heart pounded with the anticipation of facing what might be one of my most challenging encounters.

Knowing the gravity of what lay ahead, I retreated to my meditation room, a space filled with ancient symbols and artifacts that I had collected over the years, each item vibrating with its own history and power. I needed to connect with the spirit world to understand the forces at play at River Run before arriving there.

I was currently single; Katie took off about a week ago. Better for me. She was a drain on my energy.

I lit several white candles and frankincense, the flickering lights casting shadows that danced across the walls, creating an otherworldly ambiance.

As I sank into a deep trance, the air around me grew chilly, and the edges of my consciousness blurred. I invited the spirits to speak, to reveal the truths hidden in the shadows of River Run.

The room filled with the sound of eerie winds, a symbolic manifestation of the spiritual storm that awaited me. Whispers snaked through the air, unintelligible at first, then growing clearer, more urgent.

Then, there he was—the entity at the heart of River Run's haunting. Not just a disgruntled spirit or lost soul, but a devilish presence, his form in my vision was a dark, swirling vortex of malevolence.

Dear God. It's the devil himself. His eyes, if you could call them that, burned with a hellish glow, piercing through the veil between our worlds. The encounter was so intense, so vivid, that I snapped out of my trance, gasping for breath, a wave of nausea overwhelming me as I wretched, the taste of bile sharp in my throat.

"You dare to trespass, David Ray?" the chilling voice echoed in the corners of my room, long after the vision had faded. "You and the witch, Sabrina, meddle in realms beyond your ken."

As I steadied myself, leaning heavily against the wall, the pieces began to fall into place. His presence was easy to push out, I was surrounded by white light and my meditation room was heavily protected.

The curse at River Run, I realized, was tied to the unjust death of a Witch Child—an innocent who had been wrongfully accused and executed, her spirit bound in turmoil and rage. "She was a witch, yes, but her death... it was unjust. She'd hurt no one. Yet," I whispered to myself, the realization chilling me to the bone.

But I knew this, as well as I knew my name. The child, a girl named Elizabeth, had been innocent when she was murdered but she was marked for evil from birth. Her mother and her mother before her had served this devil. And yes, I knew his name but I didn't want to use it. Or share it with anyone.

The implications were clear and dire.

If the curse was fueled by such a profound injustice, its influence over River Run was not just a haunting—it was a malignant, vengeful force that sought retribution.

And now, with a young girl like Kim present, it was active, desperately seeking to rectify past wrongs through any means necessary. Armed with this knowledge, I knew what needed to be done.

Sabrina and I would have to confront this dark history head-on, to untangle the web of deceit and death that had ensnared River Run.

As dawn broke, casting a pale light through the windows of my meditation room, I prepared to leave for River Run, my resolve hardened.

The battle to protect Kim and lift the curse would be daunting, but I was ready.

History, spirits, and devil be damned—we would set this right. I packed my tools, my books, and my protective amulets, ready to face whatever awaited at that cursed place. The road ahead would be fraught with danger, but it was a path I had to walk, for an innocent child.

After packing my tools and protective amulets, I settled back into my meditation room for one more session before setting out for River Run. The previous vision had left a residue of cold fear, but also a burning need to confront whatever lay in wait.

With deep, measured breaths, I grounded myself, surrounding my spirit with layers of protective energy that shimmered in my mind's eye.

Once again, I sank into the trance, deeper this time, letting the currents of the spirit world pull me along. The room's temperature dropped as if ice had replaced the air, a physical manifestation of the spectral storm I was tapping into.

My body felt detached, floating in a space where only spirits and echoes exist. Some people call it the astral realm. I never know what to call it, except the Other Place.

The eerie winds returned, now carrying whispers that were more demanding, more coherent in their chilling messages. The shadows in the corners of the room gathered like spectators, their forms flickering and undulating with each gust of ethereal wind. It wasn't long before the entity revealed itself again—not through sight, but as a pressing darkness that filled the room, oppressive and thick.

"You come to me again?" The voice of the devil, laced with scorn and malice, reverberated around me. It was more than a voice; it was a force, attempting to invade my thoughts, to instill terror. "The child is destined to serve, as her lineage decrees. You cannot change what is written in the dark."

Struggling against the overwhelming presence, I focused on the essence of the curse, the unjust death of Elizabeth. "She was a child, misled by forces she didn't understand," I argued, my voice firm despite the spectral pressure. "Her death was a mistake, one born of fear and ignorance, but her killer has been long dead. You've twisted her fate into something dark."

A low, menacing laugh echoed through the room, chilling me to the bone. "Ignorance and fear are tools, used well by those who know how. She serves me now, as all her line have. What can you offer against such eternal servitude?"

"I offer you nothing!" Gathering all my psychic strength, I pushed back against the dark tide, affirming my intent not just to communicate but to challenge and change the narrative that had been set centuries ago. "Release her and end this cycle of vengeance. Let the child go, and let the living find peace."

The room fell silent, the winds ceasing abruptly as if cut by a knife. The darkness receded slowly, reluctantly, leaving behind a heavy stillness. I emerged from the trance, exhausted but enlightened.

The devil's words, though twisted, had revealed much about the nature of the curse and the depth of his claim on Elizabeth's spirit.

Knowing the weight of what awaited at River Run, I prepared myself for the journey. The drive would be long, and the battle longer still, but armed with the knowledge of Elizabeth's true story and the devil's intent, I felt a grim determination settle over me.

This wasn't just about banishing a ghost or calming restless spirits. It was about righting a wrong that had festered in the dark, about freeing a soul ensnared by ancient malice, and protecting a living child who might otherwise fall into the same shadowed fate.

I packed my car and set off for River Run, ready to confront whatever awaited, armed with resolve and the tools of my trade.

Arriving at River Run under the dimming light of late afternoon, the estate loomed ominously before me, its windows like dark, watchful eyes. The air around the house felt thick with tension, as if the very atmosphere was charged with unseen currents.

Sabrina greeted me at the front door, her expression grim but resolute. Mike and Sophie were there too. Their faces said it all. They'd almost lost their lives, and their child, in this house.

"I'm so glad you came," she said, stepping aside to let me in. "The activity has intensified since last night. It's like he knows we're onto him."

"He does," I assured her coldly.

Inside, the house was a nexus of anxious energy. Wen and May, looking weary and worried, nodded in greeting. Hiding behind them was a beautiful little girl. She had shoulder length dark hair, chunky bangs, and expressive eyes. My heart sank at seeing here. I couldn't even offer a smile. Sophie and May sat on either side of her, Mike and Went settled on the opposite couch.

"Thank you all for coming," Wen said, managing a strained smile. "We're all set for whatever needs to happen."

I nodded, setting down my equipment—satchels filled with salt, crystals, and various talismans that might help in cleansing the house. I spent a few minutes encouraging them to be positive, think positive. Try not to fall into the trap of negativity. "If you think we'll fail, we will."

Everyone agreed and said they understood. I took them at their word. "First, I need to see the most affected areas. Sabrina says Kim's room is a hot spot. I'd like to start there," I stated, already sensing the darker swirls of energy that permeated the air. "I can feel there is also a significant location outside."

Sabrina led me to Kim's room, where the atmosphere was notably colder, the remnants of spiritual turmoil palpable in the air. "This is where the presence of the Witch Child is strongest," she whispered, as we stepped inside. "If I had to guess, I'd say, there is a portal in this room. It's usually in a closet or a window but it may not be limited to that."

I took a moment to center myself, then began to unpack my tools, arranging them in specific patterns on the floor. As I lit a circle of white candles around us, the shadows seemed to recoil slightly, as if repelled by the light. I breathed a sigh of relief. That was something at least.

"Let's begin," I declared, my voice steady but resonant, echoing slightly against the old walls of Kim's room as I began to chant.

The room was charged with an almost palpable energy as I readied myself to recite the protective incantation, a key element in fortifying our defenses against the pervasive darkness at River Run. The candles flickered as I drew a deep breath, grounding myself in the present, focusing on the here and now, the physical space that needed shielding.

As I began to chant, my voice steady and clear, the words of the incantation resonated deeply within the walls of the room:

"Guardians of the watchtower of the east, spirits of air,
I call upon thee to shield us from evil and despair.
Encircle us with your mighty gale,
Let not this malevolence within our circle prevail."

With each line, the air seemed to thicken, charged with ancient power, the words weaving a barrier more robust than steel, more impervious than any physical wall.

*"Guardians of the watchtower of the south, spirits of fire,
Grant us your ardor, your divine pyre.
Burn away deception, light our night,
With your blazing might, set this right."*

The candles blazed up as if answering the call, their flames leaping high, casting long, dancing shadows against the walls, as if the fire itself was eager to combat the darkness that encroached upon us.

*"Guardians of the watchtower of the west, spirits of water,
Flow through this space, let your strength not falter.
Wash over us with your purifying waves,
Drown out this evil, protect these brave."*

A coolness swept through the room, like the refreshing touch of a gentle rain, washing over us, cleansing the air of the palpable dread that had thickened it before.

*"Guardians of the watchtower of the north, spirits of earth,
Ground us in your strength, prove your worth.
Build around us your unyielding fort,
Hold fast against this malevolent sort."*

As the final words of the chant echoed through the room, I could sense the malevolent presence recoiling, frustrated by the formidable barriers now in place.

The protective circle glowed faintly with an ethereal light, visible only to those attuned to the spiritual plane, a clear sign that our defenses were set, our wills aligned against whatever darkness sought to breach them.

"Is it over?" May whispered to Wen who had no answer. I didn't have the heart to tell them that we hadn't even gotten started yet. Those invocations were just for protection, and hopefully they held up during the battle to come.

With our protections in place, we were better prepared to confront the entity, to challenge its claims and break its hold on River Run. The battle would be arduous, the risks great, but armed with ancient wisdom and spiritual guidance, we stood a chance to restore peace to this troubled place.

Yeah, he was just waiting to get in.

As the ritual deepened, the room seemed to pulse with power. Whispers slithered around us, emanating from the shadows, growing in intensity. They were not just whispers but hisses, spitting malevolence and ancient spite, forming words that threatened and warned.

A disembodied spoke and the sound of it shook the very air. "You cannot break what has been ordained. This child will fulfill her destiny." Each word was a knife, slicing through the air with chilling precision. As if to accentuate the threat, the remaining candles blew out.

Sabrina and Sophia acted swiftly, her hands moving deftly in the dark to relight the candles, her movements practiced and sure. As light returned, it seemed to push back against the palpable darkness, a visual struggle between light and shadow playing out before our eyes.

The newly lit flames danced wildly, as if reluctant to stay alight, their flickers casting grotesque shapes against the walls that seemed to move of their own accord.

This entity, this ancient devil, was not merely a ghost or a lingering spirit; it was a force of ancient evil, bound to the land by chains of tragedy and blood. Our battle was not just with a spirit, but with history itself, with the very darkness that it had spawned.

"Elizabeth Kelly! I call on you to reject the devil! Reject the curse he has placed on you! Step forward and into the light and you shall be forgiven. You shall be free!" Sabrina shouted at the ceiling.

We steeled ourselves, ready to push harder, to chant louder, to break through the veil and challenge the fate it claimed was unchangeable. We waited to hear something from Elizabeth but did not hear a word.

The air felt like a battleground, charged with the echoes of a thousand lost souls, and tonight, we were their champions, their voices. The smart thing, some would say, would be to send the family away while Sabrina and I did our work but it was important that the Lee and Boyson families attend. I wanted them all to feel stronger.

"Fine. Your destiny is your own to choose," I countered loudly, the room temperature dropping as the battle of wills intensified. "But you have no claim here, bound to the past by wrongs that can be righted. Kim Lee is not of the Kelly line! You cannot claim her!"

I could feel invisible hands around my neck. The entity's anger was palpable, a physical pressure that made it hard to breathe. But amidst the oppressive darkness, I sensed a flicker of something else—uncertainty, perhaps, or the dawning realization that the devil's hold here might indeed be broken.

As I struggled to breathe, my fellow medium tried to help me. "Elizabeth Kelly! I know you're here! You were just a child when you were killed. We're here to offer peace," Sabrina added, her voice strong and clear. "To you, and to the other children. All the others that died. Nobody has to suffer. Not even you. You can be free, Elizabeth Kelly!"

The invisible hands released me but I wasn't ready to quit.

The session stretched on, each minute a contest of spiritual strength. We maintained our chants, our calls for peace and release, the room occasionally shaking with the force of the entity's resistance.

"In the name of God, we break your curse! We break your ties here! We break the cords that bind you to this place!" Sabrina and I began to chant the mantra again and again, the two families joined us.

Finally, the air began to lighten, the oppressive feeling lifting slowly as if a weight was being removed from the room.

Exhausted but hopeful, we ended the session, the silence that followed feeling like the first calm after a tempest. The shadows seemed less menacing, and even the air felt easier to breathe.

"We've made some headway," I said, packing away my tools. "But we'll need to maintain the barriers and continue the pressure. This was just the beginning."

Wen and May, visibly relieved yet still tense, nodded their understanding. "We'll do whatever it takes," May said, her voice firm. "For Kim."

As we stepped out of the room, the house felt different—still shadowed, but less hostile.

The battle for River Run was far from over, but for the first time, there was a glimmer of real hope. The night ahead would be crucial, a test of the ground we'd gained and the resolve we brought to bear against the darkness clinging to this old, haunted place.

That night, after an exhausting day of spiritual battle, I collapsed into the modest bed provided by the local inn near River Run.

The darkness of the room seemed to echo the lingering darkness at the estate, but exhaustion quickly pulled me under into a deep sleep.

However, rest was elusive; the spiritual entities we were contending with at River Run had not finished with me yet.

In my dream, the landscape morphed into a distorted version of River Run, with shadows twisting into grotesque shapes under a blood-red sky. The ground beneath my feet felt unstable, like walking on a thin crust over a churning abyss.

As I navigated this nightmarish realm, I soon encountered the Witch Child, Elizabeth Kelly. Her appearance was spectral, her eyes glowing with an eerie light, her expression a mix of sadness and fierce determination. Once she had been a lovely little girl with a future but she'd been marked before birth.

I worked my way slowly toward her in the astral realm. She spoke, her voice carrying the weight of centuries of grief and anger. "They seek us, those with the gift. The gifted females are the ones he desires most, to serve his dark purposes. My unjust death was the seed that let him root here, a door he now uses to reach for others like me. I cannot stop him and neither can you!"

As Elizabeth's spectral form hovered before me, behind her materialized the dark, devilish entity—a shadow darker than the night around us, with eyes like coals burning in the deep.

"She served me in life, and now in death," his voice boomed around us, the ground trembling with his power. "I seek a return, a new vessel to continue my work. The curse will draw them here, to me, until I find the one who can sustain my presence, to serve me again."

The entities' words revealed a chilling truth: The curse at River Run was not just a residual haunting or a spirit bound by unfinished business. It was a calculated trap, set by a demon using the unjust death of a young witch to tether his presence to the physical world, targeting families with potentially gifted female children to find a suitable host.

Elizabeth's face showed a glimmer of remorse amidst her anguish. "Bring the girl so I can live again. If you do not, he will destroy you all."

Waking from the dream, the images and voices still ringing in my ears, I felt a renewed sense of urgency and horror. We were not just fighting to save a young girl from a haunting; we were battling to prevent a powerful demon from continuing a cycle of death and possession.

I gathered my thoughts and prepared for the day ahead. Armed with the knowledge from my dream, I knew our strategy at River Run had to be twofold: free Elizabeth from her bindings and prevent the demon from achieving his goal.

The stakes were higher than ever, and the battle would be unlike any other I had faced.

After a brief, restless pause to gather my bearings following the vivid dream, I met with Sabrina and the Lees in the dimly lit living room of River Run. The morning light struggled to penetrate the thick, oppressive atmosphere of the house, casting long, gloomy shadows against the walls. Kim was sitting at one end of the couch coloring in her many books but I knew she was listening to every word. She had to know she was in danger.

Poor kid. I prayed to God she would make it.

Chapter Ten—May

As the late afternoon sun dipped lower in the sky, its fading light stretched the shadows across the old orchard into long, dark fingers that seemed to claw at the ground. I led David Ray along the narrow, overgrown path that wound its way towards the heart of the orchard, where the infamous witch tree stood like a sentinel of the past.

The air around us was thick with chilling expectancy, and I pulled my sweater tighter around myself, warding off the cool breeze that carried whispers of forgotten times. Wen and I exchanged glances, but I didn't feel comforted by looking at him.

David walked with a purposeful stride, his eyes keenly surveying the gnarled branches and thick underbrush that flanked our path.

"The energy here is tumultuous," he said, his voice low but clear enough to carry over the rustling leaves. "This orchard isn't just a place where things happened; it's a repository of all the emotions, all the dark events that have been absorbed by the soil and the trees. For hundreds of years, blood has soaked the ground here."

The rest of us—Wen, Sophia, and Mike—exchanged uneasy glances, our own apprehension mirrored in each other's faces. The orchard felt alive, as if it breathed in our fears and breathed out an eerie, unsettling calm.

Every step seemed to stir up more than just the fallen leaves; it felt as though we were walking through the remnants of all the sorrows that had unfolded here.

As we approached the witch tree, its imposing presence loomed over us, its branches gnarled and twisted unnaturally, as if writhing in silent agony. The ground beneath it was barren, a stark circle where nothing grew, as though the earth itself was blighted by the tragedies tied to the tree.

David Ray stopped a few feet away from the tree and turned to us, his expression solemn. "The dolls were found here, hanging from the branches. It's no coincidence—it's as if the tree itself is a marker, a gravestone for the untold stories and unquiet spirits that refuse to rest."

"How did you know that?" I asked curiously. I felt a shiver run down my spine; the memory of the dolls tangled in the limbs haunted me. The thought that Kim had been drawn to such a place, even unknowingly, filled me with a deep, maternal dread.

"Understanding this place," David continued, breaking into my thoughts, "is key to unraveling the curse. We must tread carefully, respect the pain and the power that saturate this ground."

The orchard around us seemed to listen, the wind rustling through the leaves as if whispering secrets back and forth between the gnarled trunks.

It was a reminder that, in this place, the past was very much alive, intertwined with the present, and we were intruders in a story that had begun long before we arrived.

The sudden silence that fell upon us as we stood under the looming presence of the witch tree was palpable. The usual sounds of the wind whispering through the leaves seemed to halt, as if the orchard itself was holding its breath, awaiting David's next words. The shadow of the tree stretched ominously across the ground, its form dark and twisted against the grass as the sun continued to sink lower in the sky.

David placed his palms against the rough, weathered bark of the tree, closing his eyes as if to sense the stories embedded within its ancient wood.

"Elizabeth Kelly's heart is buried right under here," he said, his voice echoing slightly in the quiet of the orchard. "This tree... it's more than just a tree. It's a conduit for the curse, a channel through which the energies are drawn up from the earth and dispersed into the air."

The rest of us gathered closer, the gravity of his revelation drawing us in. The idea that the innocent young child, Elizabeth, was buried beneath this very spot made the air feel heavier, as if her spirit was still entwined with the roots, trapped in perpetual unrest.

"This tree needs to be removed," David continued, opening his eyes and looking at each of us in turn. "It's a focal point for the curse, a pillar that holds up the veil between the living and the dead. As long as it stands, the curse has a stronghold, a physical anchor in this world."

Wen furrowed his brow, visibly troubled by the notion. "Remove it how?" he asked, looking from the tree to David. "Do we cut it down? Burn it? I'm pretty sure I'll have to get a permit to remove it. It's got to be at least three hundred years old."

Before David Ray could respond, the air around us shifted. A cold gust of wind swept through the orchard, rustling the leaves and sending a shiver down my spine.

The atmosphere thickened, and I could almost feel the resistance from the spirits tied to this place.

"Neither," David Ray replied, his gaze fixed on the tree. "Maybe remove it isn't the right word. We need to bind the evil to this tree so it can't escape. If we burned it, such actions might release a burst of evil energy we are not prepared to handle. We need a more controlled approach, a ritual that can sever the ties without causing harm to the spirit of Elizabeth or to us."

The decision seemed to weigh heavily on him, his usual confidence tempered by the seriousness of our task. It was clear that the path forward would be fraught with challenges, each step needing careful consideration and respect for the forces we were dealing with.

What was he not telling us? I got the feeling that the mediums knew more than what they were telling us.

The clouds above us were suddenly swollen and menacing, rolled in with unnatural speed, blotting out the remaining slivers of sunlight. The air grew heavy, charged with an electric anticipation that sent a collective shiver through us all.

David paused, looking skyward, his expression grim. "The storm isn't just weather; it's a manifestation," he murmured, almost to himself but loud enough for us all to hear. "The energy we're stirring up is resonating with the natural elements. It's an awakening forces we need to be prepared to contend with."

No sooner had he spoken than a low rumble of thunder growled across the landscape, a sound so deep and resonant it seemed to vibrate in our chests. The wind picked up, whipping around us, carrying with it the scent of rain and something else—something ancient and rooted in the dark soil beneath our feet.

It was as if nature itself had turned against us. Wen clutched my hand protectively.

Lightning forked across the sky, illuminating the orchard in stark, fleeting glimpses of white light that threw the gnarled shapes of the trees into grotesque relief. Each flash seemed to reveal hidden forms—shadows within shadows—that moved just beyond the edge of vision, retreating into the darkness as quickly as they appeared.

Wen grabbed my hand, his grip tight. "We should get back to the house and check on Kim," he said, his voice barely audible over the mounting wind that howled through the trees, causing the old branches of the witch tree to sway and creak ominously.
The tree seemed to be alive, reacting to our presence and the rising storm with a malevolent anticipation.

As we hurried back towards River Run, the first drops of rain began to fall, heavy and cold, splattering against the leaves and the ground with a sound like whispers.

"Run, everyone!" Sophia shouted as if any of us needed to be told. The rain grew quickly into a deluge, soaking us within moments, plastering our clothes to our skin and hindering our visibility as we navigated the increasingly muddy path.

The storm escalated rapidly, the wind howling like the cries of the lost souls that lingered in the orchard, as if the spirits of the past were voicing their unrest. The thunder was relentless now, a continuous roar that seemed to shake the very ground, punctuated by sharp, bright flashes of lightning that tore across the heavens.

I glanced back once, compelled by a mixture of fear and fascination, to see the witch tree silhouetted against the stormy backdrop, its branches thrashing as if caught in the throes of a fierce struggle.

For a moment, it appeared as though the spirits of the tree were reaching out towards us, desperate or angry, or perhaps both.

As we rushed through the rain-soaked orchard, the atmosphere suddenly thickened with more than just the storm's fury.

A rustling, distinct from the wind's howl, rose from the deeper shadows of the woods.

One by one, spectral figures materialized between the gnarled trunks of the ancient trees. The apparitions of young girls, dressed in the tattered remnants of another era, their faces pale and drawn, their eyes hollow with unspoken tragedies.

The figures moved with an eerie, deliberate slowness, their limbs jerky as if unused to motion. Each step seemed measured, purposeful, and their numbers grew as the storm intensified around us.

My breath caught in my throat when I saw one spirit in particular—a girl with a chilling resemblance to Kim. Her dark hair plastered around a face too solemn for a child, her eyes searching, hauntingly familiar. The sight was a visceral blow, rooting me to the spot for a heart-stopping moment.

The eerie procession of spirits began to advance towards us, their movements gaining an unsettling momentum. Their expressions, vacant yet intent, suggested a malevolent purpose as they drifted closer, pushed by the storm's energy.

"Back to the house!" David Ray's voice cut through the tumult, urgent and commanding. The reality of our danger snapped me out of my shock, and I turned, clutching Wen's hand tightly.

Our feet slipped and slid on the muddy ground as we ran, the spectral figures' slow pursuit seeming to keep pace with the storm's rage.

The wind screamed in our ears, a banshee chorus that mixed with the softer, more sinister whispers of the spirits. It felt as though the orchard itself was alive, animated by the storm and the dead.

Lightning flashed again, a strobe that illuminated the relentless pursuit of the spectral girls, their faces eerily calm amid the chaos.

We dashed through the torrential downpour, the house of River Run finally coming into view through the sheets of rain. The old building looked like a sanctuary, its lights a beacon against the dark fury of the night.

My lungs burned with the cold air, and the ground beneath our feet became increasingly treacherous as the mud thickened.

Reaching the safety of the porch, we slammed the heavy door shut behind us, the sound echoing like a gunshot in the now-silent house. Leaning against the door, we caught our breath, our hearts pounding not just from the run but from the fear of what had followed us.

The howl of the wind seemed almost a wail of frustration from the spirits left outside, thwarted by the barrier of the house's walls.

Inside, the dimly lit hallway of River Run felt like a different world compared to the wild chaos of the orchard. But the relief was short-lived; the danger outside had not dissipated, it merely lurked, waiting.

We exchanged glances, each of us understanding the gravity of what we faced. Not only did we have to contend with a physical storm but also a supernatural one, each feeding into and intensifying the other. The night was far from over, and our battle to protect Kim—and ourselves—had reached a new, more desperate level.

We barely managed to close the heavy front door of River Run against the storm's wrath. The solid thud of the door shutting reverberated through the house, a stark contrast to the chaos outside. Inside, the atmosphere was tense, each of us catching our breath, our minds reeling from the encounter. "We can't just cut it down," Wen gasped, his back against the door as if he could physically keep the horrors at bay. "Not without understanding more... not with them guarding it."

I nodded, feeling the weight of his words. The spirits linked to the witch tree weren't just remnants of the past; they were active guardians, perhaps bound to protect the curse or Elizabeth herself. "It's not just about removing a tree or appeasing a spirit," I murmured, trying to piece together our next steps. "It's about understanding the ties that bind them here. We need a solution that respects the depth of what we're facing."

As we gathered our wits, Sophia and Mike joined us, their faces etched with concern. They had stayed behind to look after Kim, ensuring she wasn't exposed to the immediate danger.

Now, they listened intently as we described the spectral procession and the storm's eerie timing. "The spirits are restless, and the storm might be their way of trying to stop us," David said, his voice firm despite the palpable unease in the room. "We need to perform the ritual tonight."

The urgency of his statement set everything into motion. There was no time to waste; the increasing activity and the storm's intensity suggested that whatever barriers we had were weakening.

"The ritual needs to be the right one—it will require all of our strength and focus," Sabrina added, pulling out her notes and the collection of ritual components we had gathered earlier.

As darkness enveloped River Run, and the storm continued to rage outside, we huddled in the living room, the only light provided by flickering candles. Their glow cast long, unsettling shadows against the walls, mimicking the restless spirits outside. We spread out the ritual diagram on the coffee table, each symbol and line chalked out with precision.

"We'll need to be precise," David instructed, pointing to each element of the setup. "Every symbol, every chant is crucial. They're not just words and drawings; they're the keys to locking this curse away."

I took Wen's hand, feeling the strength of his grip, and looked around at the determined faces of my friends and family. "We'll do it together," I declared, my voice steadier than I felt. "For Kim, and for every spirit that Elizabeth's curse has trapped here. We end this tonight."

That was the first bit of hope I'd felt in a long time, and I latched on to it.

The resolve in the room solidified like a shield, each of us drawing strength from the other. We were no longer just a group of frightened individuals; we were a united front, ready to face whatever the night brought.

Outside, the wind howled like a beast thwarted, but inside, we prepared to reclaim peace for our home and for the spirits caught in an endless cycle of sorrow and rage.

Tonight, the battle was not just against a storm or a haunted past, but against a darkness that had seeped deep into the very foundations of River Run.

Chapter Eleven—David

Inside River Run, the living room, which had become the designated ritual room, felt like a calm amidst the storm raging outside.

I gathered everyone—May, Wen, Sophia, and Mike—and laid out the blueprint of our strategy on the old oak table that now served as our command center. Kim was present too but we did our best to keep her occupied with other things, like puzzles, toys and snacks.

The room was dimly lit, the only light coming from candles placed strategically around the room, casting long, dancing shadows against the walls.

"I need everyone to understand their role clearly," I began, my voice steady despite the undercurrent of urgency that ran through it.

I unfurled a scroll containing ancient symbols and diagrams, each representing elements of the ritual we were about to perform. "This isn't just about severing unwanted ties; it's about reclaiming power and protecting Kim from forces that seek to misuse her potential."

I pointed to the symbols, explaining their significance. "These are not just drawings; they are ancient seals that will help us fortify our space and keep the malevolent energies at bay. I need to draw these symbols on your hands and feet, Kim. It won't hurt but it might tickle a little. Is that okay?" I asked the little girl.

She didn't hesitate but put her hands out. Her mother seemed nervous, but I was grateful she didn't stop me. I drew the symbols on her feet too.

The wind howled like a beast outside as we continued with the ritual. The room's atmosphere felt charged, a tangible tension filling the air as if the house itself was aware of what was about to transpire.

I directed the group to position sacred objects: crystals at the cardinal points around the room, herbs like sage and salt scattered in a circle around us, and ancient symbols marked on the floor with white chalk.

"Each of these elements plays a crucial part in our defense and the efficacy of the cord-cutting," I explained, my hands methodically arranging the symbols with precision. "The circle will serve as our fortress, the crystals our sentinels. The herbs purify and protect, while the chalk lines bind our intentions to the earth."

As I lit the final candle, the storm outside seemed to respond, a loud crack of thunder echoing as if in challenge. I took a deep breath, feeling the weight of the moment.

"Let's begin," I said, looking around at the anxious faces of the group. "Keep close, follow my lead, and focus on your intentions. We're going to go back in time, we have to go back and see the initial connection. Once we know how the cord was attached to Elizabeth, we'll know more. It might help us to know how to break it."

As we settled into the rhythm of the ritual, the candles casting a protective glow around us, I guided the group into a deeper state of concentration.

"Focus on the source of the connection," I instructed, my voice low and steady. "We need to see the origin, to understand how to sever it."

As the ritual intensified, the air within the room thickened as if reality itself were warping, the fabric of time stretching into a dense, oppressive haze. It felt as if the very essence of the room was dissolving, and suddenly, I was no longer within the safe confines of River Run but transported to a dimly lit, ancient cabin from centuries past.

The room was sparse, illuminated only by the guttering light of tallow candles that cast flickering shadows upon rough wooden walls. Around me, a hushed assembly of cloaked figures encircled a small, crudely made cradle.

Inside, a newborn girl lay, her eyes wide and impossibly deep, reflecting a soulful intensity that belied her age. It was Elizabeth Kelly, unmistakable, the sorrow already set within her gaze.

An elder, cloaked and hooded, stepped forward with a grave solemnity that filled the air with a heavy, ominous dread. In his hand, he held a small bowl filled with a dark, thick substance—blood.

Yes, I could see this all quite clearly. I had the feeling that Sabrina could see it too.

With deliberate reverence, he dipped his finger into the viscous liquid and approached the infant. The room held its breath as he traced a complex sigil upon Elizabeth's forehead.

The sigil pulsed with a malevolent crimson light, contrasting starkly against her ghostly pale skin, imbuing the scene with an eerie, otherworldly glow.

The cold touch of dread deepened as I watched, unable to move or intervene.

The elder's voice, deep and resonant, began to chant in a tongue that felt both ancient and forbidden, each syllable a heavy stone in the fabric of the night.

As he spoke, the assembled figures murmured their agreement, a chorus of low, haunting echoes that seemed to seep into the very walls of the cabin. Their faces, illuminated briefly by the candlelight, were etched with a mixture of fear, awe, and blind devotion.

As the chant reached its crescendo, the blood sigil on Elizabeth's forehead throbbed with a dark light, and a palpable wave of energy surged through the cabin, making the air shiver and the candle flames dance wildly. The elder's final words seemed to seal an invisible pact, binding the infant to a fate far beyond the ordinary.

Oh, God. This is black magic at its worst. At its very worst.

Snapped back to the present, the vision fading like smoke, I was left gasping, the echo of the ancient chant still ringing in my ears.

Shaken, I turned to the group, their faces blurred for a moment as if through a veil of water.

"This curse... it's bound by blood, woven into her very essence from birth," I managed to say, my voice a rasp of dismay and urgency. "Breaking it is not just a matter of dispelling a spirit or cleansing a house. It's about undoing a pact sealed with the most primal forces we know. It's going to be complex, challenging, and dangerous."

The group absorbed the gravity of this new knowledge, their faces reflecting the mix of fear and determination that filled the room. Sophia reached out a comforting hand, her touch grounding, reminding me of the support we shared.

Despite the daunting revelation, we pushed forward with the ritual. "I know now what binds Elizabeth," I said, rallying the group's spirits. "Blood. The blood of the entire coven. And with that knowledge comes power. We can break this cycle, but it requires everything we have. Elizabeth did not consciously decide to join this coven, to do the demon's bidding. If we can convince her to resist him, we can win."

The storm outside seemed to crescendo with our efforts, thunder clashing with our chants, lightning illuminating the room in stark flashes that mirrored the intensity of our task.
May rose to her feet. "What if she doesn't? What if she doesn't resist the demon? Shouldn't we just leave? Just move?"

Sabrina and I exchanged glances. "It won't do any good. She's marked and they will come for her. She is indeed a natural witch."

"What does that even mean?" May asked as she hugged her daughter, and they cuddled on the couch. Wen drew close to his wife and daughter.

I smiled at the child to try and ease her fears. "A natural witch is someone born with abilities that others don't have. A natural witch knows how to heal, intuitively. She'll know what herbs to use. She'll know how to make things grow, even bring things back to life. Small things, like birds. It's a good thing, usually but when a natural witch gets the attention of the darkness, well…"

The candles flickered wildly, as if struggling to maintain their light against a suffocating darkness that pressed in on us. Shadows moved at the edge of our vision, forms and whispers materializing in the corners of the room, challenging our resolve. I immediately began scribbling on the floor with the sacred chalk.

With one last, powerful incantation, I directed the group to focus all their energy on the sigil we had drawn—the symbol of severance.

The room shook as if the very foundation of the house was being challenged. A ghostly wail filled the air, and for a moment, Elizabeth's spirit appeared before us, her face contorted in a mix of anguish and hope.

"Release me," she whispered, her voice carrying the weight of centuries. "Come with me, Kim. If you come with me, I can go."

"No!" May shouted at her. "You cannot have her!"

"Please! Help me! Set me free! Only you can set me free, Kim! Please!" She reached for the living child. Elizabeth appeared the picture of loveliness with golden hair and pale skin.

"NO! She's not leaving! She cannot set you free! You have to do it! Tell him no, Elizabeth! Tell him no! Everyone! Say it with me. Tell him no!"

With a collective shout, we completed the chant, and the sigil on the floor blazed with a pure, white light.

The oppressive atmosphere broke like a fever, the air suddenly clear and the room brightening as if a heavy veil had been lifted. Exhausted but heartened, we slumped back, the ritual complete but the impact of our actions yet to be fully realized. The candles steadied, their light now steady and calming.

We exchanged looks of weary triumph, knowing we had done all we could to right the wrongs of the past.

"We wait now," I said, my voice hoarse but hopeful. "We wait, and we watch, and we hope that our efforts have brought peace to Elizabeth, to Kim, and to River Run."

As the storm outside began to ebb, so did the tension in our shoulders. We had faced the darkness together, and now, under the clearing skies, we dared to hope for dawn.

May breathed a sigh of relief. "Everyone, please. Stay with us tonight. It's late and this storm isn't going to let up anytime soon. Please. There is plenty of room."

We readily agreed. I opted for the living room couch while Sabrina took one of the upstairs bedroom. Somehow, despite the storm raging outside, we found peace inside.

Eventually, I fell asleep.

Chapter Twelve–May

In the aftermath of the ritual, as the last echoes of the storm faded into a quiet murmur outside, River Run seemed to exhale a long-held breath of tension.

The house, with its sprawling rooms and shadowed corners, no longer felt like a cage wrought with whispers and watchful eyes. There was a lightness, a lifting of the oppressive heaviness that had draped over us like a suffocating veil. I helped tidy up the living room, we left the drawings on the floor, just in case.

I helped my daughter bathe and put on her favorite pajamas.

The morning light filtered through the windows with a clarity that hadn't touched these walls in weeks, casting gentle patterns on the wooden floors and painting the air with a hopeful luminescence. The usual creaks and groans of the old structure sounded more like the comfortable settling of a weary beast than the restless stirrings of a haunted one.

Wen, Sophia, Mike, and I shared a quiet breakfast, the first in a long while where the weight of unseen eyes felt absent. We exchanged tentative smiles, the kind born from a battle endured together, and there was an unspoken agreement in our glances—a hope that perhaps we had turned a corner, that maybe, just maybe, the nightmare had loosened its grip on our home.

After breakfast, with the deceptive calm hanging over River Run, the decision was made for the Boysons, David Ray, and Sabrina to leave.

Their presence over the past few days had been a beacon of hope and strength, but now, as the immediate threat seemed to abate, they needed to return to their own lives, carrying with them the weariness and the scars of the battle we had all shared.

David clasped my hand firmly before he left, his gaze searching mine for any signs of lingering fear. "You call me, day or night, if anything feels off," he instructed with a stern kindness that made me feel both comforted and more alone.

Sabrina, with her quiet strength and reassuring smiles, hugged me gently. "You've got a strong spirit, May. Trust in that. Trust in the work we've done here," she whispered.

The Boysons, Mike and Sophia, looked exhausted but managed weak smiles as they packed their car. "We're just a phone call away," Sophia reassured, her eyes shadowed with the remnants of her own family's ordeal echoing ours. "Keep an eye on Kim, and on each other," Mike added, his tone serious, reflecting the gravity of what we'd experienced. "Come out and see us, Wen. We're just on the other side of town and the kids love the swimming pool."

As their cars pulled away from the driveway, the sense of normalcy they took with them left a stark emptiness behind. I stood there, watching them disappear down the road, feeling the weight of the house looming behind me, its quiet more pronounced without their presence.

Turning back to the quiet of River Run, I knew I had to keep vigilant.

The ritual had brought us a momentary peace, yes, but the shadows of doubt lingered, as did the memories of the horrors we'd faced. The relief of their departure was tinged with an isolating realization: from here on, we had to protect this peace, this semblance of normalcy, on our own.

Despite the outward calm, I found myself unable to sleep, my mind reeling from the night's events. The images of the ritual, the brief appearance of the Witch Child's spirit, and the intense energy of the confrontation left me restless.

Each creak and whisper of the house in the night sounds magnified, fueling my anxiety and keeping me awake.

Driven by a growing sense of unease that clung to me like a cold shadow, I found myself unable to remain confined within the walls of River Run any longer. The house, though quieter, now seemed to echo with whispers of its turbulent past, each noise sharp against the backdrop of silence.

In the depths of night, unable to quell the restlessness that tugged at my senses, I slipped from the warmth of my bed and the quiet breaths of Wen beside me. In the half light, I studied him. Yes, I still loved him, despite his faults.

Pulling a heavy sweater around my shoulders, and sliding thick slippers on my feet, I ventured out into the cool night air.

The moon above was a thin crescent, barely shedding light on the path that led to the orchard, where earlier rituals and confrontations had unfolded. My feet knew the way, carrying me almost unwillingly through the darkness, the shadows of the trees casting gnarled patterns on the ground.

The air was thick with the scent of earth and something faintly bitter, like the remnant of burnt herbs.

As I approached the orchard, a prickling sensation crawled up my spine. The corn cob dolls, those eerie harbingers, hung from the branches once more, swaying slightly in the gentle night breeze.

I expected this, didn't I?

Their presence was impossible—hadn't we removed them? Hadn't we cleansed this place? Yet here they were, arrayed like macabre ornaments, their button eyes gleaming dully in the moonlight, reflecting back my own fear.

A shudder ran through me as I stepped closer, my heart pounding loud in the stillness. The dolls seemed to watch me, their stitched mouths twisted in silent sneers or pleas—I couldn't tell which.

The air around them felt charged, as if they were not merely inanimate objects but vessels, imbued with a purpose I dared not comprehend fully.

I reached out tentatively towards one, the closest that dangled from a low branch, its body twisted unnaturally by the wind. Just as my fingers brushed the coarse material of its dress, a sudden chill swept through the orchard, the wind picking up, whispering through the leaves with a sound much like laughter or crying.

I couldn't be sure.

Pulling my hand back as if burned, I took a step away, my breath visible in the air before me as the temperature seemed to drop. The night had turned hostile, the once familiar path now a labyrinth of shadows and threats.

My own home, which was supposed to be a place of refuge, seemed a lifetime away in that moment, separated by an expanse of darkness that was both physical and palpable in its menace.

With one last look at the unsettling figures that hung like specters of River Run's troubled past, I turned and hurried back towards the house, the uneasy feeling of being watched accompanying me every step of the way.

As I neared the safety of the lit windows, the sense of something amiss lingered, a foreboding that what we had tried to end was perhaps only just beginning.

Shaking from the chill and the eerie encounter in the orchard, I stepped back into River Run, hoping for the warmth and safety of its walls.

Yet the sense of unease that had haunted me outside followed me indoors. As I closed the door behind me, a sickening sense of dread settled over me like a heavy cloak.

Ugh. I hate this house. We weren't staying here. I didn't care what Wen said.

The dimly lit hallway, usually welcoming and familiar, now seemed alien and menacing. My heart skipped as I noticed something out of place—a shadow, or a shape, that hadn't been there before.

My eyes adjusted to the low light, and I froze. Hanging from the stairway banister, the back of chairs, and along the hallway were the corn cob dolls. They were positioned deliberately, their button eyes staring blankly, their stitched smiles twisted in grotesque mimicry of cheer.

Am I dreaming? Please tell me I am dreaming!

Each doll seemed to have been placed with careful intention, creating a tableau that mocked our efforts to cleanse and protect the home.

Panic surged through me, icy and sharp. The realization that the dark forces we thought we had banished were not only still here but boldly asserting their presence was terrifying. This was no random placement; it was a clear, chilling message that the battle was far from over.

I angrily snatched them down and threw them in the garbage can. I wept as I did so but I was careful not to wake up my family. We'd all been through enough and apparently, it wasn't over.

Exhaustion weighed on me, but sleep was a stranger in my bed that night. My mind churned with the haunting images of the dolls and what they represented.

Wen lay beside me, his breathing deep and even, the very picture of peace in contrast to the storm inside me.

As I lay there, the shadows in the room deepened, coalescing into a form at the edge of the bed.

A figure, dark and indistinct, materialized from the gloom. It leaned towards me, its presence oppressive and chilling. The figure spoke in a whisper, but it filled the room, a voice both seductive and terrifying.

"May," it murmured, its tone dripping with dark promises, "imagine the power to right all wrongs, to punish the betrayer. It does not skip a generation, but you've shut out your gifts. I can help you. I can make you strong. Stronger than your mother. I can teach you to protect her."

"You lie!" I whispered in the dark. "Everything you say is a lie!"

"Do you think he loves you? He made love to her, the other woman. What was her name? Carly? Carla? I can show you how to get vengeance."

"How can you know that?"

It was speaking of Wen, his past indiscretions that still stung. "He has wronged you, hasn't he? Betrayed your trust? Wouldn't you like to make him feel as you have felt?" The words were venom, tempting and horrible, preying on my deepest hurts and darkest thoughts. "Wouldn't you like to punish him?"

"Get out! Get out of my house! Now! Get out!"

I reached out, shaking, to wake Wen, needing him to banish the nightmare unfolding before me. But he was unresponsive, his body unmoving, his breaths shallow as if held in thrall by the same dark power that now whispered seditions in my ear.

Panic and fear mingled with the dark allure of the figure's words. But somewhere, deep down, a stronger part of me rebelled against the darkness.

The prayer Goldie had taught me surged forth in my mind, a beacon of strength. I began to recite it silently, gathering every shred of will against the dark temptations.

As the prayer strengthened, the figure recoiled, its form wavering as if in pain.

"No!" it hissed, the room growing colder with its fury. But the sacred words were stronger, and slowly, the shadow dissolved into the air, leaving a lingering cold in its wake.

Breathing hard, I finally managed to rouse Wen, the normalcy of his waking presence a stark relief against the terror of the night. We clung to each other, the remnants of the ordeal fading as we reaffirmed our bond, our unity a shield against the dark.

In the quiet aftermath of the spectral visitation, Wen stirred beside me, his eyes flickering open to the dimly lit room, now silent and still.

The oppressive presence had vanished, but the chill lingered, a reminder of the darkness that had tried to seep into our sanctuary.

Wen's gaze found mine, clouded with confusion and concern as he sensed the residual tension in my posture, the fear that hadn't quite left my eyes.

"What happened, May?" he murmured, his voice thick with sleep but sharp with worry. "Is it Kim?"

He sat up, his hand reaching out to cup my face, his touch warm against the cool air. The

familiarity of his touch, the concern in his eyes—
it all helped to anchor me back to the reality of
our bedroom, away from the shadowy edges
where fear still lurked.

I leaned into his hand, allowing myself a moment
to just breathe, to feel the safety his presence
brought. "It came back—the darkness," I
whispered, the words tasting bitter. "It tried to
tempt me, to turn me against you, using your
past, our past. He wanted...he wanted me to
betray you!" I spilled my guts, speaking in our
native tongue, hoping against hope that
whatever might be listening would not
understand.

Wen's expression tightened, the muscles in his
jaw clenching as he absorbed the weight of my
words. "I'm so sorry, May," he said, his voice
breaking slightly. "For everything. For the pain
I've caused you. For bringing us here. For trying
to escape my responsibility. I am sorry. Truly
sorry."

The honesty in his voice, the raw regret for the
wounds we'd both inflicted on each other over
the years—it was all laid bare in that quiet,
vulnerable confession.

My eyes welled up, not just from the fear of what
had happened but from the understanding that
this man beside me was battling his own
demons, just as I battled mine.

"I forgive you, Wen," I said, the words coming out stronger and more certain than I felt.

"Really?" He sat up and wiped his dark hair from his tear-filled eyes.
"Really. I love you, and I know the man you are now is not the man who made those mistakes. We've both grown, we've both learned."

Tears spilled over as I spoke, tracing warm paths down my cheeks. Wen pulled me close, his arms wrapping around me tightly, as if he could shield me from any more darkness that might dare to come close. His own tears mingled with mine, a silent acknowledgment of the pain we'd endured and the healing that was still taking place.

"We'll get through this, together," he whispered into my hair, his breath warm against my scalp. "Whatever comes, we face it together."

And there, in the quiet of our room, with the remnants of a storm and a nightmare slowly fading into the past, we held each other.

It was a moment of forgiveness, of healing, a reaffirmation of our bond that no shadow could truly sever. As we wept together, it wasn't just from fear or pain, but from a shared strength, a knowing that together we were whole, unbroken, and resilient.

This healing moment marked not an end, but a new beginning—a recognition of the battles we'd fought, both separately and together, and the battles we'd continue to face.

But for now, in each other's arms, we found peace.

With deliberate movements, I unbuttoned my pajama top and slid it off my body. Wen did the same. We fell back on the pillows, immediately began kissing and to my great relief, I did not see the other woman in my mind's eye. I saw only us. Only me and Wen.

We made love until the sun rose and collapsed into a peaceful sleep.

I woke up once, suddenly. I thought I heard a noise, a sound but I must have been imagining things. I'd sent the devil away and sealed my future with my husband. There was nothing in this house. River Run was free, so were we.

I'd made up my mind and made my decision. Family first and that was all that mattered.

Wen was not without his faults but I did forgive him. I did and I would. Hopefully, this will never happen again. I prayed against it.

I kissed his cheek as he slept and soon I fell back to sleep too.

Chapter Thirteen—Wen

The sun dipped below the horizon, casting long shadows across the lawn of the colonial home, a sense of foreboding settled heavy in the air, as palpable as the evening mist that began to curl around the base of the old trees.

Inside, the house seemed to pulsate with a life of its own, the walls creaking more than usual, the floors groaning under the weight of a sinister presence that grew stronger each night. It had been a week since David Ray and Sabrina's work had been done and even though we hadn't seen anything, I knew things weren't right.

You could just feel it. Even though May had forgiven me and we'd made beautiful love together several times since then, it always felt as if we were being watched. I didn't like that feeling.

I stood out the kitchen window, watching as darkness took hold, the light fading as if swallowed by the growing evil outside and within these walls. A strange aroma passed by me. I knew that horrible smell.

The devil's presence was no longer just a whisper or a fleeting shadow; it had become an oppressive force, testing our defenses, looking for any weakness to exploit. May was feeling the presence too, but we didn't talk about it. It was almost as if we spoke about it, it would manifest.

The air inside grew inexplicably cold, and I could see my breath as I exhaled, watching it mingle with the chilly air that had seeped in uninvited.

Sounds began to emerge from the corners of the house, subtle at first—a distant banging like a door repeatedly slamming shut, the shatter of glass that sent shivers down my spine, and a low, incessant hum that seemed to come from the very foundation of the house.

I turned away from the window, trying to shake the eerie feeling creeping over me, when suddenly, the lights flickered violently. I jumped, my heart racing as shadows danced across the room, thrown by the unstable light that struggled against the encroaching darkness. Then, as quickly as it had begun, the house plunged into darkness, the only light now coming from the moon, casting ghostly silhouettes that played against the walls like specters roaming the halls.

The silence that followed was deafening, heavy with expectancy, as if the house itself held its breath. Then, almost in response to my own heightened fear, the floorboards upstairs began to creak loudly, as though bearing the weight of something unseen moving with deliberate, heavy steps. The sound descended the staircase, each step thudding ominously, coming closer, yet when I strained my eyes towards the darkened hall, nothing appeared.

Gathering my courage, I called out, "Who's there?" My voice echoed strangely in the empty house, swallowed by the shadowy corners. No answer came, only the sound of my heart pounding in my ears and the distant rumbling of thunder outside, a storm brewing as if summoned by the night's dark turn.

I was glad my family wasn't home. They'd gone to pick up supper and some ice cream. I now wished I'd gone with them.

The atmosphere was thick with dread, every creak and rustle magnifying my fear. It was clear the devil was making his presence felt, showing us that despite our efforts, despite the rituals and the prayers, he was not so easily banished.

The devil was here, pressing against the spiritual barriers we had erected, clawing his way in, desperate to reclaim what he believed was his.

When May and Kim returned, the sight of me standing pale and shaken by the door instantly brought a rush of concern to May's face. "Wen, what's wrong? You look like you've seen a ghost," she asked, her voice laced with worry as she balanced the bags of takeout and ice cream in her arms.

I shook my head, trying to dismiss the heaviness that clung to my chest. "Something's not right," I managed to say, glancing around the dimly lit foyer as if expecting the shadows to move. "The house... it's worse tonight. I heard things, felt things. We can't stay here."

The fear in my voice was enough to make Kim clutch her mother's side, her small face buried against May's leg. We all moved into the living room, setting down our dinner uneaten as the room seemed to close in around us.

"We need to talk about what we're going to do," I said as we gathered around the old coffee table, our usual spot for family discussions. The flickering light from the fireplace cast eerie patterns on their faces, highlighting the mix of fear and resolve etched deeply into their expressions.

May was the first to break the heavy silence. "I tried calling the Boysons earlier, hoping they could offer some advice or help. No answer." Her voice was tight with frustration, her eyes reflecting the flickering firelight. "I left messages, but it's like they've vanished. I didn't call Sabrina or David Ray, but maybe we should. What do you think?"

I shook my head. I had no fight left in me.

The reality of our isolation pressed in on us, the silence from the Boysons serving as a grim reminder of our situation. The discussion that followed was tense, a back-and-forth between trying another ritual, with the uncertainty and risks it entailed, and the overwhelming desire to flee, to leave River Run behind before darkness claimed more than just our peace.

Kim, her voice small but filled with a child's clear insight, said, "I don't like it here anymore, Mommy. Can we go? What if the girl comes back?"

Her words seemed to tip the scales. Looking into the eyes of my family, seeing the fear and the fatigue from the battles we'd already fought, the decision became painfully clear.

"Yes. We should leave," I declared, the weight of leadership feeling heavy on my shoulders. "Tonight, if we can. It's not safe for us here anymore—not for any of us."

Reluctantly, but with a growing sense of inevitability, we all nodded in agreement. The idea of leaving our home, the life we'd built, was heart-wrenching, but the danger of staying was far worse. The decision was made. It was time to leave River Run, to seek safety and perhaps one day, a new place to call home.

The silence that followed our decision was filled with a mixture of relief and sorrow, each of us lost in our thoughts about the home we were leaving behind and the uncertain future that lay ahead.

"Kim, go pack your backpack. I'll come up and help you in a minute."

As we scrambled to gather our essentials, the atmosphere within River Run seemed to thicken with hostility. Shadows curled around the edges of the rooms, as if watching our frenzied efforts to flee. The air was punctuated by an uneasy silence, broken only by the sound of drawers slamming and the rustle of clothing being stuffed into bags.

Suddenly, a cold gust swept through the house, as if the front door had been flung open to the night. But I knew it hadn't—it was something else, something far more sinister.

"Kim!" Was all I could say as I waited to hear her call back. She didn't.

Then, there came a breeze; it was like a wave of ice water, sending shivers down my spine and extinguishing the few lamps we had lit to guide our way. The house plunged into darkness, and with it, a heavy weight of silence fell. I could hear a transformer pop outside.

I fumbled for my flashlight, my hands shaking as I switched it on, casting an unstable beam of light across the room. May was right beside me.

"Kim? Kim, answer me!" I called out, my voice echoing oddly against the walls, as if absorbed by the darkness.

No reply came, just the sound of our own hurried movements. Then, a door upstairs slammed with such force it shook the walls. Another door followed, then another, like a violent cascade throughout the house.

Amidst this chaos, a scream—Kim's scream—pierced the air, short and sharp, then abruptly muffled.

"Kim!" May shouted, terror sharp in her tone. We both raced toward the stairs, tripping over the bags we'd packed in our haste. Upstairs, the hallway was a black tunnel, the flashlight beam doing little to penetrate the oppressive dark.

"Kim!" May yelled again; my voice desperate. We checked her room, the bathroom, the spare room—every possible corner she could have squeezed into. But there was no sign of her, no whispered replies, just the suffocating silence that seemed to mock our fears.

The realization that Kim was nowhere to be found set in, panic sharp and biting. It was as if the house had swallowed her whole. "No! Kim! Where are you, honey?"

May's face was stricken, her eyes wide and fearful as we met in the hallway, the beam of my flashlight flickering between us.

"She was supposed to get her backpack," May gasped, her voice breaking, "I should have come with her. How could she just disappear?"

The notion that something within River Run had taken her—that the house we had tried to make a home had turned against us so completely—was overwhelming.

We called her name over and over, our voices growing hoarse, as we searched each room again, refusing to give up hope. But with each passing minute, the eerie silence of the house seemed to grow denser, heavier, as if absorbing our fear and transforming it into something palpable.

We needed to find her, to bring her back from whatever corner or shadow had claimed her. The urgency was a palpable force, driving us forward despite the fear that clawed at our hearts. The search for Kim became a desperate mission, each of us splitting up to cover different parts of the house with a growing sense of urgency and dread.

Every closet was flung open, every bed was checked under, and every corner scanned. But the silence that met each call for Kim was chilling, the house seemingly empty but for our own panicked movements.

Realizing the futility of our search inside, we burst out into the cold night air, our breaths creating misty clouds as we raced towards the orchard. The place had a notorious feel by now, a sinister chill that seemed to emanate from the very soil.

The witch tree, that monstrous, gnarled behemoth, loomed in the dim moonlight, its branches swaying slightly as if in greeting.

As we approached, the sight of the corn cob dolls hanging from the limbs struck a new wave of terror in our hearts.

How is this possible? How?

They swayed eerily, each one a grotesque parody of a child's toy.

Among them, I spotted the doll that bore an uncanny resemblance to Kim. It hung there, eyeless face staring blankly into the night, its presence an ominous sign that made my heart sink.

Unable to contain the horror and despair that surged through her, May fell to her knees beneath the tree, the damp earth cold and unforgiving. Her hands dug into the soil, a sob tearing through her as I grasped the doll, pulling it down from its noose.

"Kim!" I cried out again, my voice hoarse, tears streaming down my face as I clutched the doll to my chest.

May and I, together with the bleak shadows of the orchard around us, continued to search. We called her name into the night, each shout a mixture of hope and fear. The orchard seemed to close in around us, the trees whispering secrets we couldn't understand, the darkness a blanket that muffled our pleas.
Eventually, we had the presence of mind to call the sheriff's department. They came quickly but there was no sign of our daughter. No sign whatsoever. Even her backpack was still on her bed. They tried to force us to stay inside and wait for her to return but neither of us agreed to that.

May and I searched the grounds right along with the rest of the deputies.

Every rustle of leaves had us turning, hearts pounding, hoping for a glimpse of her, for any sign of her presence. But the orchard gave up no secrets, holding its breath as we searched, the moments stretching into an agonizing eternity.

The realization that Kim might truly be lost to us, possibly taken by the very forces we'd fought so hard to banish, was a weight too heavy to bear.

How do we explain to the detectives what had been happening here? I had no idea.

As the search dragged on through the night, with officers combing the shadows and flashlights piercing through the darkness, the chilling silence of the orchard became oppressive.

Each call for Kim echoed back unanswered, a stark, hollow sound that seemed to mock our desperation. The deputies' voices grew less hopeful, their movements slower, as the reality of the situation sank deeper into everyone's minds. Eventually the Boysons joined us, hugging and consoling us. Doing their best to help us find our daughter. I was grateful for their support but also angry. Why had this happened to Kim? I didn't want anything to happen to the Boyson child but our Kim was young and innocent.

Just a little girl. A girl in the clutches of the devil.

The sheriff approached us, his hat in hand, a grim expression on his face. "We've covered the grounds, checked every possible spot. There's no sign of her," he said, his voice heavy with the weight of his words. "We'll keep looking, keep teams here as long as it takes, but... you might want to prepare yourselves for all possibilities. Are you sure you aren't forgetting something? Maybe a stranger hanging around? Any weirdos?"

His words hung in the air, a sentence left unfinished but understood. "This whole house is weird," I answered sharply. "Our daughter is gone! Please, help us find her!" He had nothing else to say. In fact, I could see it in his eyes, she wasn't going to be found. She was gone. They knew about this place. They knew about River Run.

Everyone had known. Except us.

May collapsed against me, her sobs muffled against my chest as I held her, my own tears mingling with hers. Around us, the night continued dark and silent, the moon a mere observer to our despair.

With dawn approaching, the harsh light began to reveal the stark reality of our situation. New search teams were coming but I was sick. So sick that I wasn't sure I could handle much more.

Sophia held May as she cried. Mike watched me but we didn't speak. What was there to say? This should have been you. No. I didn't mean that and I sure wouldn't say it. Tears flowed down my face but I couldn't bring myself to make a sound.

The house stood ominously quiet, as if it had retracted into a watchful stillness, its secrets locked away in the shadows. The devil had stolen my daughter. These fools would never be able to find her. In the meanwhile, Mike got on the phone with David Ray and Sabrina. They both made their way to the house but they could offer no help. The police questioned them, asked them about their time at the house, their interactions with Kim but they were both cleared pretty quickly.

Days turned into a week, then weeks turned into months.

"It's my fault," I whispered, the words slicing through the night like a confession. "I brought us here. I thought... I thought we could make it work."

May shook her head, tears streaming down her cheeks as she looked up at me. "We did everything we could, Wen. This house, it's... it's something else. It's not just a place. It's as if it's alive, and we woke up something terrible."

The bitter realization that Kim was forever lost to us, potentially taken by the very entity we'd hoped to banish, felt like a physical blow.

I could see in May's eyes the same fear that was clawing at my heart—the fear of never again hearing Kim's laughter, of never seeing her bright eyes light up in excitement, of never holding our daughter again.

"We can't stay here," I said, my voice barely above a whisper, but resolute. "We have to leave. For Kim, for us. We have to find a way to move on, even if it means leaving a part of our hearts here."

"We can't leave her. She's here. She'll come back, Wen! She'll come back!" She sobbed and I held her. I didn't bother reminding her that David Ray and Sabrina could offer us no further help.

They'd tried to reach out, tried to make contact but it was as if the Other Realm had shut the door on us. We would never get her back.

The devil got his due and we'd been powerless to save her.

As the days stretched painfully into weeks with no sign of Kim, the atmosphere around River Run grew heavier, a tangible sorrow filling every corner of the once cherished home. Despite the endless efforts and countless searches, hope dwindled with each passing day, until the unbearable decision was made: we could not stay here any longer.

Before we left, driven by a visceral need for closure, May ventured out to the witch tree one last time. The early morning mist clung to the ground as she walked alone, the air thick with the scent of earth and old leaves. The sky was a bleak grey, mirroring the turmoil within her. I followed her, without her knowing. I didn't trust her to be on her own.

The orchard was silent as she approached the witch tree, its branches heavy and still as if mourning. It stood there, an ominous sentinel in the fog, the memories of our nightmarish discoveries beneath it haunting May's every step.

Her breath caught in her throat as she drew closer. So did mine. Where once the corn cob dolls had swayed ominously, there was now an eerie stillness.

The doll that resembled Kim, which had hung there as a macabre token of her presence, was gone. In its place, something far more horrific took shape through the mist. I blinked, unbelieving what I was seeing.

Kim's small, lifeless body hung from a branch, her favorite dress tattered and her limbs at unnatural angles. The sight was so grotesquely unthinkable, so brutally final, that May's knees buckled beneath her. She fell to the cold, wet ground, her hands clawing at the dirt as an epic wail of agony escaped her lips. The sound echoed through the orchard, a heart-wrenching cry that resonated with the grief of a mother who had lost everything.

The wail pierced the morning stillness, traveling through the trees and reaching the empty house, leaving a trail of despair in its wake.

Around her, the world seemed to pause, the wind holding its breath, the birds silent, as if nature itself mourned with her.

May's grief was all-consuming, a physical pain that tore through her chest with each shuddering sob. She cried out again, her voice hoarse, calling to the daughter she would never hold again. Her tears mingled with the mud, her sorrow seeping into the earth beneath the cursed tree.

I held her, her body wracked with sobs, her spirit shattered. I was numb and found that I could not speak.

Gently, I pulled May into my arms, trying to shield her from the cruel truth that lay so plainly before us. Together, we mourned under the shadow of the witch tree, our cries a lament for Kim and for the life we had lost.

And now another horrible gathering of police officials herded around the house. Questions were asked. Insinuations made. The investigation revealed Kim had only died within the past twenty-four hours. We had no idea where she'd been but when they did their investigation, they found our daughter's body broken, bruised and bloodless. We had no answers, only the weight of an unbearable loss.

Our departure from River Run became a silent exodus, a departure laden with defeat and heartbreak. We left behind not just a home, but our souls, forever entwined with the dark legacy of the land.

As we drove away, the house and the tree faded into the distance, becoming nothing more than bleak silhouettes against the gray sky.

River Run was behind us now, but the shadows it cast were long and dark, reaching far beyond the boundaries of its cursed grounds, a reminder of the darkness that had consumed our lives and taken our beloved Kim.

I didn't realize then, as I drove May and myself away from River Run the full extent of the tragedy that would unfold. My wife could not bear the heartache. She decided to leave this life, forgetting me completely.

When I found May's body, cold and stiff in the bathtub, I was shattered beyond repair.

And I would remain so. Like many others who came to River Run, we never truly escaped.

I lost everything: my daughter, my wife, my very soul. I buried May but along with her, I buried my heart.

And that's where it remains to this day.

Epilogue–Carmen

The house stood ominously quiet, its imposing structure casting long shadows over the unkempt lawn as the sun began to set. Inside, I waited by the window, my expression composed and a small, knowing smile played on my lips.

The air around me felt charged, as if anticipating the arrival of the new family—a family with four daughters, any of whom could potentially please my master. Oh, that's all I wanted to do. Please my master. I could feel his approval.

The crunch of gravel announced their arrival, and I watched as the station wagon pulled into the driveway. The Baggett family, unaware of the house's dark history, were eager, their faces bright with the prospect of a new home. I smoothed my skirt and prepared my warmest welcome, stepping onto the porch just as they gathered their things.

"Welcome to River Run," I said as they approached, my voice as inviting as the house was foreboding. The parents, Mr. and Mrs. Baggett returned my greeting with enthusiastic smiles, their daughters glanced around with wide-eyed curiosity.

I led them inside, letting them explore the rooms freely. The house felt alive again, its halls echoed with the sounds of potential victims—the laughter and footsteps of a family about to unknowingly entwine their fate with its cursed legacy.

Mrs. Baggett lingered by the fireplace, a flicker of concern crossing her features. Smart woman, this one. But not smart enough. Certainly not as smart as I was but then again, few were.

"Why did the last family move out? Please tell me the truth," she asked, her voice tinged with a hesitancy that suggested she was not sure she wanted to know the answer.

"A tragedy," I responded with a practiced sigh, my tone one of subdued sorrow. "Their young daughter passed away, a horrible accident. An accidental hanging. Not in the house, in the woods. But that's all in the past now. They've moved on, and the house is ready for new memories. Happy memories. Did you know that this is one of the oldest houses in Fairfield?"

As they continued their tour, I stepped out onto the porch, where the air was cooler and the fading light cast long shadows across the ground. Beside the car, invisible to anyone but me, stood a figure clad in all black, his features handsome yet devoid of warmth.

My master.

He nodded slightly, his dark eyes scanning the house with an intensity that sent a shiver down my spine.

"This family is acceptable," he murmured in my mind, his voice a low whisper that only I could hear. "One of the daughters has the abilities we need. Unlike the last one, she will value the gift."

I nodded, understanding the weight of his approval. "Yes, master," I replied, my voice barely above a whisper.

"Pardon?" Mrs. Baggett asked. I hadn't heard her high heels come up behind me.

As the family returned to the porch, their faces alight with excitement and plans for the future, I couldn't help but feel a twinge of something akin to regret. They had no idea what lay ahead, what this house would demand of them.

But it was not my place to warn them, only to prepare them. No one warned me. Not even the man that supposedly loved me and abandoned me.

I watched the Baggett family drive away, their station wagon disappearing down the long driveway, taking them one step closer to their new life at River Run—a life that will undoubtedly be woven into the fabric of tragedies that the house collected.

Yes, I would hear from them soon. Mrs. Baggett was a greedy woman. I sensed that about her. I recognized it. She wanted River Run. Wanted to possess it and the history that came with it. Wanted to enjoy it.

My smile faded as I turned back into the house, the door closing behind me with a soft click, sealing away the secrets and the darkness until it was time to claim its next victim.

I knew I didn't have long to wait.

Author's Note

Dear Readers,

Thank you for joining me once again on a journey back to River Run, a place where the shadows whisper and the past never truly dies. "Witch Child," the third and final installment in the River Run series, invites you to unravel the deeper, darker mysteries that began with the historical Fairfield Witch Trials.

In this book, we follow the Lee family as they grapple with a legacy of curses and hauntings that test the bounds of their courage and their hearts. It's a story about the lengths we go to protect those we love, the past's stubborn grip on the present, and the heavy price of secrets long buried.

Crafting "Witch Child" was a journey through the cobwebbed corners of history and horror, blending fact with fiction to keep the shadows at bay (or perhaps to invite them in). This book is a continuation of a narrative that, like River Run itself, is built layer by layer—each one darker and more intricate than the last.

I hope this tale captures your imagination and haunts your dreams in the way only a good ghost story can. For those of you who have been with me since the beginning, thank you for your continued enthusiasm and support.

And if this is your first time visiting River Run, beware—the ghosts of the past are eager to tell their tales.

Prepare to be chilled, thrilled, and perhaps a little bit haunted.

Yours in storytelling,

M. L. Bullock

PS. You can email me at authormlbullock@gmail.com. If you'd like a signed paperback, visit my website at MLBullock.com. I also have an active social media presence on Facebook. I hope to hear from you or see you there!

M. L. Bullock's Book List

If you think you've missed one of my books, here is a comprehensive list of everything and they are IN ORDER.
 All books are available on Amazon Kindle, and as paper books. Some are available as audiobooks.

SEVEN SISTERS
#1 Seven Sisters
#2 Moonlight Falls on Seven Sisters
#3 Shadows Stir at Seven Sisters
#4 The Stars That Fell
#5 The Stars We Walked Upon
#6 The Sun Rises Over Seven Sisters
#7 Beyond Seven Sisters
Bonus Christmas at Seven Sisters
Bonus The Ghost on the Swing
Bonus Silent Night, Haunted Night
The Ultimate Seven Sisters Collection

IDLEWOOD
#1 The Ghosts of Idlewood
#2 Dreams of Idlewood
#3 The Whispering Saint
#4 The Haunted Child
The Hauntings of Idlewood

RETURN TO SEVEN SISTERS
#1 The Roses of Mobile
#2 All the Summer Roses
#3 Blooms Torn Asunder
#4 A Garden of Thorns

#5 Wreath of Roses
Return to Seven Sisters Collection

THE GRACEFIELD HAUNTINGS
#1 Haunted Gracefield
#2 The Three Graces
#3 Grace Before Dying
The Gracefield Hauntings Collection

MARIETTA
#1 The Bones of Marietta
#2 Footsteps of Angels

THE BEAUMONT SAGA: A SEVEN SISTERS PREQUEL
#1 Olivia
#2 Louis
#3 Christine
The Beaumont Saga

A SEVEN SISTERS MYSTERY
#1 Haunted Halls of Rosegate Manor
#2 Ghostly Echoes at Wysteria House
#3 The Howling at the Sycamore Hotel
#4 The Screamer of Stuckey Asylum

DEVECHEAUX ANTIQUES AND HAUNTED THINGS
#1 A Cup of Shadows
#2 A Voice From Her Past
#3 A Watch of Weeping Angels
#4 The Ghost Mirror

#5 The Phantom Lamp
#6 The Darkening Door
#7 Kalliope's Dollhouse
#8 The Mourning Heart (2024)
Devecheaux Antiques and Haunted Things Trilogy Volume 1
Devecheaux Antiques and Haunted Things Trilogy Volume 2

SUGAR HILL
#1 Wife of the Left Hand
#2 Fire on the Ramparts
#3 Blood By Candlelight
#4 The Starlight Ball
#5 His Lovely Garden
The Sugar Hill Collection

THE GHOSTS OF SUMMERLEIGH
#1 The Belles of Desire, Mississippi
#2 The Ghost of Jeopardy Belle
#3 The Lady in White
#4 Loxley Belle
The Ghosts of Summerleigh

SOUTHERN GOTHIC SERIES
#1 Being With Beau
#2 Death's Last Darling
#3 Spook House
The Southern Gothic Collection

WELCOME TO DEAD HOUSE
#1 Never Dead
#2 Always Dead
#3 Dead at Midnight
Welcome to Dead House Series

HAUNTING PASSIONS
#1 For the Love of Shadows
#2 Her Haunted Heart
Haunting Passions

GULF COAST PARANORMAL Season One
#1 The Ghosts of Kali Oka Road
#2 The Ghosts of the Crescent Theater
#3 A Haunting on Bloodgood Row
#4 The Legend of the Ghost Queen
#5 A Haunting at Dixie House
#6 The Ghost Lights of Forrest Field
#7 The Ghost of Gabrielle Bonet
#8 The Ghost of Harrington Farm
#9 The Creature on Crenshaw Road
#10 A Ghostly Ride in Gulfport
#11 The Maelstrom of the Leaf Academy
#12 The Ghosts of Phoenix No 7
#13 The Ghosts of Oakleigh House
#14 The Spirits of Brady Hall
#15 The Gray Lady of Wilmer
Bonus The October People (A Gulf Coast Paranormal Extra)

GULF COAST PARANORMAL TRILOGY
#1 Ghosted
#2 Haunted
#3 Spooked
#4 Dead
#5 Paranormal
#6 Delta Hex
#7 Delta Dead
#8 Shadowed
Gulf Coast Paranormal Season One Boxed Set
Gulf Coast Paranormal Season Two Boxed Set

GULF COAST PARANORMAL SEASON TWO
#1 The Wayland Manor Haunting
#2 The Beast of Limerick House
#3 The Haunting at Goliath Cave
#4 The Skeleton's Key
#5 Death Among the Roses
#6 The Spiritus Mirror
#7 The Captain of Water Street
#8 Return to the Leaf Academy
#9 The Rising of Lucy Vallow
Bonus Horror Ever After (A Gulf Coast Paranormal Extra)

GULF COAST PARANORMAL SEASON THREE
#1 Tower of Darkness
#2 Haunted Molly
#3 The Children's Playground
#4 Lullabye for the Dead
#5 Ship of Darkness
#6 The Biloxi Banshee

TWELVE TO MIDNIGHT
#1 Mary Twelves
#2 Pieces of Twelves

BRYNN LEEDS HAUNTING
#1 We Walk in Darkness

MORGAN'S ROCK
#1 The Haunting of Joanna Storm
#2 The Hall of Shadows
#3 The Ghost of Joanna Storm
The Haunting at Morgan's Rock Trilogy

QUEEN MUMMY
#1 Queen Mummy

RIVER RUN
#1 River Run
#2 Blood Run (2023)
#3 Witch Child (2024)

SOUTHLAND
#1 Southland
#2 Southland: Legacy (2024)
#3 Southland: Reborn (2024)

THE DESERT QUEEN
#1 The Tale of Nefret
#2 The Falcon Rises
#3 The Kingdom of Nefertiti

#4 The Song of the Bee Eater
The Desert Queen Collection

LOST CAMELOT
#1 Guinevere Forever
#2 Guinevere Unconquered
#3 The Undead Queen of Camelot
Lost Camelot Trilogy

SHABBY HEARTS (A Romantic Comedy Series)
#1 A Touch of Shabby
#2 Shabbier By the Minute
#3 Shabby By Night
#4 Shabby All the Way
#5 Star Spangled Shabby
#6 A Shabby Wedding (Coming in 2024)

MISCELLANEOUS
Ghosts on a Plane
Dead Is the Loneliest Place to Be
After Ella
Ghosts of the Atlantis

BY MONICA BULLOCK
Delivered Me From Evil

Made in the USA
Coppell, TX
14 June 2024